Nate

ROCKS

the

BOAT

Karen Pokras Toz

Published by

Grand Daisy Press

ISBN-13: 978-0-9848608-1-4
ISBN-10: 0984860819

Library of Congress Control No: 2012934648

For more information, please visit
www.karentoz.com

Edited by With Pen in Hand
Cover and Interior Design by BookStarter

Manufactured in the United States of America

Praise for Nate Rocks:

"This book is right up there with 'Middle School: Worst Years of My Life' and 'Diary of a Wimpy Kid'...both authors better keep an eye on Ms. Toz."

-Anne B. for Reader's Favorite

"This book is perfectly created for the middle grade reader...It was like I was right there, alongside Nate, experiencing each and every up and down he was going through. And, I enjoyed every minute!...Definitely recommended for children or the child hidden in all adults."

-Ritesh Kala's Book Reviews

"Your kids will love riding along with Nate as he jumps from one adventure to the next. They'll enjoy every minute of it, because quite simply, Nate Rocks!"

-D. Robert Pease, Author Noah Zarc: Mammoth Trouble

"Author Karen Pokras Toz has a definite five star winner right here. Nate more than ROCKS! Great book for kids of all ages and for parents too. Characters that are true to life and a story that will definitely make you smile, laugh and endear you to one smart and talented young man named NATE!"

-Fran Lewis, Author and Radio Talk Show Host

"A great book that I wouldn't hesitate to recommend to anyone. On a scale of one to five I would give this book a six because it's just that good."

-Brenda C. for Reader's Favorite

"Karen Pokras Toz captures the adolescent imagination perfectly in Nate Rockledge. Even if you're an adult, I bet you'll be grinning at the end."

-Kristy James, Author

"This is a fascinating and fun story that middle grade boys are going to love. Toz definitely has a finger on the pulse of this market. She knows what's exciting to them and uses it to create a page-turner that will leave them wanting more."

-The Children's and Teen's Book Connection

For my family—thank you for your endless love and support.

A special thank you to J & S—your many summer camp adventures proved to be quite inspirational.

Chapter 1

"But why, Mom?"

Mom barely looks up from her newspaper as I use my spoon to push the cold rubbery oatmeal to the sides of the bowl, trying to make it look like I have eaten more than one spoonful. Now is not the time to get on Mom's bad side.

"I *like* going to Oak Hill Day Camp. Tommy and Sam are there, we have pizza on Fridays, and I don't have to see Abby." Oops. Did I just say that last part out loud?

Two months ago, when we returned from our disastrous trip to Florida, my sister Abby was super nice to me. Well, nice as far as fourteen-year-old sisters go. After all, I did save her from drowning in the ocean. After we were back, she let me pick what shows we watched on television, she offered to help with some of my chores; she even let me use the bathroom first in the morning. Her loving sister act lasted for all of five days before the pre-Florida Abby started slowly creeping back. By the end of the second week, it was Miss Cranky Pants as usual.

I study Mom's face and realize by her squinting eyes that I probably should have kept that last comment to myself.

"Nathan, we've been over this a hundred times already. Dad has an opportunity to teach at a college in the mountains for the summer, and I need to take care of Grandma while Aunt Stella is on her cruise. I am going to be driving back and forth too much to have you home with me. You will love overnight camp! The mountains are beautiful in the summer. Besides, Dad will only be one town away if you need anything. Now finish your breakfast."

Mom gets up from the table and leaves the room. If I hurry, I can get all of this oatmeal down the garbage disposal, grab a cereal bar, and head up to my room before she gets back. I run to the sink as the clock ticks.

I shut my bedroom door, cereal bar in hand, proud that I managed to complete my first covert mission of the day. I even escaped the wrath of Abby. *Regular* Abby is bad enough, but Abby in the *morning* is just cruel and unusual punishment for any ten-year-old to have to bear.

What is it with older sisters? I thought thirteen was bad; well, fourteen is even worse. On any given day, I am guaranteed to hear four things: complaints, screams, whining, and tears—all from my lovely sister who thinks she knows more than any other living being.

Enough about Abby. What I really need to be thinking about is how to get out of spending my summer at overnight camp instead of being here with my friends. There has to be a way. I start to pace back and forth when I see my math book out of the corner of my eye. Shoot! I promised Dad I would finish my homework first thing this morning.

Last night, I had begged Dad to let me stay up to watch the new episode of "The Adam and Erik Show." Adam and Erik are these two brothers who get to do all sorts of cool stuff together, like hang out at the movies and ride their bikes anywhere they want. I wish I had a brother. Anyway, Dad agreed, and now I only have fifteen minutes to get my homework done before the bus comes.

I sit down at my desk and open the workbook. Fractions—ugh! I feel like we've been doing fractions forever. I get it already...make the bottoms the same...add the tops. I finish my homework with barely a minute to spare and pack up my school bag.

"Mom, I'm leaving!" I yell, as I race down the stairs. "Mom, I'm late! Gotta go!"

I stop when I reach the front door. I think I hear her yell, "Bye." Maybe she is in the shower. Usually she opens the door for me and tells me to have a nice day, but she has been letting me be a bit more independent lately. Anyway, I need to leave now, or I'm going to miss my bus. "See you after school, Mom!" I yell in one final attempt and race down the street toward the bus stop.

When I get to the corner, my best friend Tommy, who always gets to the bus stop before I do, is not there. Instead, two other boys who have their backs toward me are waiting at the corner. *New kids*? I don't remember a house for sale in the neighborhood recently. I wonder where they came from.

The boys turn around right as I get to the corner.

"Adam and Erik?" I ask in disbelief. "You're the kids from that TV show! What are you doing here?"

"Nate! Thank goodness you're here! We need your help!"

"My help? What do you need?"

"Nate, our producers want to bring in a third character. You know a long lost cousin or something, but all the kids auditioning for the show are *awful*. If the producers take on one of them, it's going to ruin us forever!" Erik explains.

"How can I help? I don't know any actor kids. Why me?"

"Why you're Nate Rocks, of course! We don't need any other actors. We need *you!* Can you imagine how awesome our show would be if Nate Rocks was our long lost cousin? Come on, they're ready to start filming!" Adam pulls my arm and starts leading me towards a wooded area behind the Caufields' house.

"Right now? But what about school? I don't know how to act! Are you sure you don't just want me to ask around at school? I'm sure there are plenty of kids from the drama club who would love to be on your show." I look back at the bus stop, still no sign of Tommy.

"You're much more exciting than those drama club kids, Nate. Besides, you don't need school. You're a star!" Erik says.

As we walk through a thick row of trees, I see a large lake surrounded by small wooden cabins. Were these always here? A big sign reads, "Welcome to Camp Kuckunniwi."

"Camp Kuckunniwi?" I ask, looking around.

"It means Little Wolf," Adams explains. "This season, we're staying at overnight camp. Isn't that cool?"

"Ah, Nate Rocks! Finally, you're here." A tall skinny man wearing jeans and a t-shirt approaches and holds out his hand. "David McHenry, the show's director."

"Hello." I shake his hand.

"Okay, boys, let's start the scene—AND ACTION!"

"But..." I say, looking around again.

Where did Adam and Erik go? I walk into one of the cabins to see them sleeping in two of the beds. A counselor is standing over them, trying to get them to wake up, but they won't budge. He looks at me.

"Nate," says the counselor. "I don't care what you have to do, but if you don't wake your cousins up and get them into the dining hall in five minutes, you all will miss going to Adventure Park this afternoon."

Adventure Park! Wow, I have always wanted to go there! I shake the boys, yell their names, do everything I can think of, but they won't budge. I go outside and find a big bucket on the side of the cabin. I run to the lake, fill up the bucket, and run back inside the cabin. They'll thank me later. *Splash!* I dump the water all over Adam and Erik. Not just a little drizzle either, those boys got a full on soaking! Adam and Erik bolt out of bed.

"Cut!" the director yells, as he rushes over to me. "Nate, that was absolutely BRILLIANT! Let's take a few minutes to dry the boys off, and we'll meet in the dining hall for the next scene."

5

Two people rush over to Adam and Erik with towels and a change of clothes.

"Sorry about that," I say, as I walk over to them. "There was no script."

Erik looks at me. "You don't need a script; you're the great Nate Rocks! Come on, they're waiting for us in the dining hall."

I follow Adam and Erik as they walk into a larger wood cabin. The first thing I notice is the smell— breakfast food! I'm not talking about mom's gummy oatmeal or mushy French toast. I'm talking about the smell of perfectly cooked eggs, bacon, sausage, and pancakes smothered with fresh butter and maple syrup. I take a seat at a table, hoping a plate of this amazing food will appear at any moment.

"Nate, are you ready?"

"Nate?"

"Nate?"

"Nathan! You're going to miss your bus already. Now stop drawing pictures all over your math paper and let's get going!"

I look up at Mom. She does not look happy with her hands on her hips and her eyes starting to bulge. I quickly pack up my bag, kiss Mom on the cheek, run downstairs, and race out the door. This time, I can see Tommy waiting for me at the bus stop.

"Tommy! Tommy!" I stammer, trying to catch my breath as I sprint towards him.

"Nathan, why are you running? You know the bus is always late."

"It's not the bus! It's summer camp!"

"Ugh," Tommy starts, "is your Mom still trying to get you to go to that stupid overnight camp?"

"Yeah," I say, getting more excited, "but I think I actually want to go."

"What? I thought you hated the idea of overnight camp."

"I did, but I'm having second thoughts, and I think you should come with me!"

"What? Why?"

"Think about it," I explain. "The whole summer with no parents around! We can just hang out and swim in the lake. I heard the counselors even let you play pranks on each other, like dumping water on each other and stuff."

I think twice about mentioning the amazing breakfasts, since Tommy's mom is actually a pretty good cook. So instead I add, "You can even eat ice cream for breakfast."

"Really?"

"Yup. Do you think they'll let you come with me?"

"What about Sam? He'll be upset if we're both not at Oak Hill Day Camp this year."

"Yeah," I agree, "but he only goes for two weeks, and then he goes on vacation with his family for the rest of the summer. We'd barely see him anyway."

"It does sound like fun." Tommy's smile grows wider.

"I'll have my mom call your mom after school today. Camp Spring Ridge, here we come!"

Chapter 2

By some miracle, Tommy's parents agreed to let him go to overnight camp with me. Sam was bummed we wouldn't be with him at day camp, but since his parents were planning a vacation to Yellowstone National Park for most of the summer anyway, he wasn't too upset. After all, he'd get to spend his summer hiking, fishing, camping...come to think of it, won't those be the same things Tommy and I will get to do at summer camp? Looks like we are all going to have fun this summer.

The last couple months of school seem to take forever. Mom decided it would be fun to have a party before we all left for camp. Sort of a going away party, I guess. Nothing big. Dad invited his boss Mr. Fisher and his wife. I invited Tommy and Sam. Abby invited her annoying best friend Emma, and Mom invited the Crane family. The Crane family consists of Mom's friend Marge Crane, her husband Ted, and their annoying daughter Lisa. Lisa is my age and has been in my class since kindergarten. She wouldn't be so bad if she could keep her mouth shut, but she is always either bragging or complaining, and she just loves to tell her Mom every time I get in trouble at school. Did I mention that her mom and my mom are best friends? Now that I think of it, Lisa is sort of like a mini Abby. Maybe she can hang out with Abby and Emma at the party, and I won't even have to see her. Nah, Abby wouldn't be caught dead hanging out with a fourth-grader. I wonder if Mom will notice if Tommy, Sam, and I sneak off to Tommy's house during the party.

"Nathan," Dad calls up the stairs, "can you come down here and give me a hand?"

"Sure, Dad."

I put away the newest edition of the Captain Asteroid comic book I'm reading and walk out of my room. I can see Mom standing in front of the mirror in her bedroom. She is trying to tie a plastic grass skirt around her waist. Just as I begin to look away, Mom turns to see me looking at her.

"Oh there you are, Nathan. Come in here." Mom finishes tying the skirt and reaches into the bag sitting on her bed. "I bought this for you to wear today." She hands me a shirt with huge bright green and yellow flowers on it.

"What's wrong with what I'm already wearing?" I look down to see my plain blue t-shirt.

"Nothing, but today we are having an Aloha party. Get it? Aloha?" I must be looking at Mom funny because she just keeps right on explaining. "You know, because we are leaving town, and Aloha means goodbye. Well, I guess it means hello and goodbye. Anyway, I thought it would be fun to have a Hawaiian theme. I have flower leis for everyone to wear as well."

"Uh—sure," I say, looking at the shirt, wondering

if there is anything I can possibly say that will get me out of wearing it. Maybe I should spill some fruit punch on it or something, then I will have to change. At least Mom bought this one and didn't try to make it herself. Her sewing skills are about as good as her cooking skills. "Thanks."

I walk back to my room and put the flowered shirt over my t-shirt. That way, as soon as Mom starts getting distracted with Mrs. Crane, I can just slip it off.

"Nathan, are you coming?" Dad yells again.

"Oh yeah, sorry, Dad. Be right there." I quickly button up the shirt and head down the steps to where Dad is waiting. I see that Mom got to him as well. He is wearing almost the exact same shirt as me, only his is pink and red.

"What's up?" I ask.

"I need you to help me outside," Dad begins. "Can you and Abby hose off all the patio furniture while I get the grill cleaned up? Everyone should be here in about an hour or so."

"Okay." I follow Dad outside. Abby is already outside, only instead of cleaning the chairs, she is sitting on a chair, in her bathing suit, sunning herself.

"I thought you were supposed to help," I say, standing over Abby.

"I did," she replied. "I cleaned this chair. Now move it! You're blocking my sun!"

"Fine," I mumble. I get the hose from the side of the house, drag it over to the chairs, and start cleaning them one by one. Dad is across the yard working on the grill. I inch over with the hose to where Abby is sitting. Should I? She *is* wearing her bathing suit, and she is supposed to be helping instead of just sitting there.

"Hi everyone!"

Before I can make a decision, I turn around to see who is talking. Great...it's the Cranes. The hose turns with me as I look over to them.

"Nathan! You're getting me soaked!" shrieks Abby, as she jumps up and pulls the hose from my hand, dropping it to the ground.

"Oops, sorry." I silently chuckle, as Abby storms into the house dripping water everywhere. At least it wasn't intentional...sort of.

Dad walks over to Mr. Crane and shakes his hand.

"Sorry we are a bit early," Mr. Crane says. "Marge wanted to give Claudia a hand in the kitchen before the rest of your guests arrive." He motions to my mom who is now walking outside. He leans over to my dad and whispers, "You know how those two are when they get together."

Dad laughs. "No problem, Ted, good to see you." He looks over to Lisa. "How are you, Lisa?"

"Fine, Mr. Rockledge," she says in that shrilling voice. "Hi, Nathan."

"Uh, hi," I mumble. "Hello, Mr. Crane."

"How are you, Nathan? You sure are getting tall."

"I am? Thanks."

Lisa and I continue to stand there in silence while Dad and Mr. Crane catch up on sports scores and grill accessories. Finally, Dad turns to me and says, "Why don't you and Lisa go play?"

Play? "Play what?" I ask. Really? Was I going to have to hang out with Lisa Crane all afternoon? Why wasn't Abby back outside yet? I'm sure Lisa would much rather follow her around.

"Well, how about horseshoes? I just set the game up in the corner over there," Dad says, pointing to the back fence. "Hey, Nathan, did I ever tell you about the time Uncle Robert and I played horseshoes?"

"You mean when you were trying to break the world record for farthest horseshoe throw, and Uncle Robert tossed it so hard it landed on Grandpop's car and cracked his windshield?"

"Yeah," says Dad with glazed eyes. "Grandpop was not happy." Dad snaps out of his "Did I Ever Tell You" trance and continues. "I bought you kids a plastic set just to be safe."

"Okay." I walk over to where Dad had setup the horseshoes, not looking back to see if Lisa was following me. Of course, she was.

"Nice shirt, Nathan."

I ignore Lisa and pile up the three green horseshoes. They seem awfully heavy for just plastic. I toss the first one and miss.

"That's not how you do it," snaps Lisa.

"I think I know how to play horseshoes, thanks." I throw the second horseshoe and miss again.

"I'm telling you…"

"Oh yeah, well if you're so good at it, let's see you try." I reach down and hand Lisa a red horseshoe.

She lifts her arm and quickly releases the horseshoe. It gracefully flies through the air, landing perfectly around the stake.

"Lucky try." I pick up the last of my three horseshoes. I concentrate, make certain that my aim is perfect, bring my arm back ever so slightly, and toss the horseshoe. It heads straight for the post...and then curves to the right missing by almost a full foot.

"Nice one," Lisa smirks. She picks up another of her red horseshoes, looks at me, and says, "You should probably move back."

"Whatever." I roll my eyes as I take a step backwards. Lisa pulls her arm back preparing to throw before I can get completely out of the way and TWHACK! Searing pain shoots through my face as Lisa slams both her fist and the horseshoe into me. I put my hand up to my face and feel the blood gushing from my nose.

"Nathan! I told you to back up!" Lisa yells.

Everything starts to spin as I sit on the ground. Why is Lisa yelling at me? She's the one who hit *me* in the face. I can see Dad running toward me.

"Nathan! Are you okay?" he asks, kneeling down next to me. "Lisa, run inside and ask Mrs. Rockledge for a towel and an ice pack."

Lisa looks annoyed and *walks* toward the house. After what seems like an hour, Mom comes running out of the house with the requested supplies. She hands Dad a towel to hold up against my throbbing nose. Mom places the ice pack over my left eye.

"Oh," she says, "that's already starting to swell and bruise."

"At least the bleeding has stopped," Dad

comments, as he removes the blood soaked towel. The sight of it starts to make me feel woozy again.

I look up and see Lisa, Mr. and Mrs. Crane, and Abby all looking down at me.

"What happened?" Abby asks.

"Nathan was too close to me when I went to throw the horseshoe. I told him to backup! None of this would have happened if he had listened to me, but he refused to accept the fact that I was beating him at horseshoes," Lisa explains with her know-it-all voice.

"You mean *you* gave him a black eye, bloody nose, *and* beat him at horseshoes?" Abby smiles down at me.

"Yup," Lisa says proudly.

I guess I won't be getting an apology from Lisa anytime soon.

"Abby," Mom says, "why don't you take Lisa inside? I'm sure she'd rather be hanging out with you and Emma today."

"Sure, Mom," Abby says without any argument. She puts her arm around Lisa's shoulder and leads her into the house. Mom and Mrs. Crane follow.

Dad helps me to a lounge chair and positions the ice pack over my face. "You should just sit here for a while Nathan and take it easy. Okay?"

I nod. Dad and Mr. Crane walk back over to the grill.

"Hey, Nathan."

I remove the ice pack from my face to see Tommy standing over me.

"Holy Cow! What happened to your face?" he

exclaims.

"Lisa whacked me in the face with a stupid horseshoe."

"Lisa Crane?" Tommy asks. "Lisa Crane gave you a black eye?"

"And a bloody nose."

Tommy clutches his stomach and falls to the ground rolling in laughter.

"It's not funny!"

"It's hysterical!" Tommy says, as he catches his breath. "What a great story you have to tell next year when the teacher asks us how we spent our summer vacation."

"What? I'm not telling anybody about this! Are you nuts?" I know Tommy is just kidding, but I am dead serious.

Tommy finally calms down and sits in the chair next to me.

"Well, what are you going to tell the kids at camp? That black eye is not going away before we leave next week."

"I don't know, I'll think of something." Tommy and I sit in silence as I try to come up with something better than a girl hitting me.

Mom walks toward us with a tray of lemonade.

"Hi, Tommy, glad you could make it," she says, handing each of us a glass. I take a big gulp and start coughing. It tastes like Mom added salt instead of sugar. She should have warned us she was serving her homemade lemonade and not the store bought brand.

"Are you okay, Nathan?" Mom asks.

"Fine, Mom." I stare at Tommy. He is still holding his glass, but he has not taken a sip yet. I try to concentrate real hard: *Don't do it, Tommy. Put the glass down. Do. Not. Drink. The. Lemonade!*

How many days until I get a break from Mom's cooking? I look over to my Dad standing at the grill and wonder if the hamburger patties that mom prepared will be safe to eat.

"Thanks for inviting me, Mrs. Rockledge."

"Of course, Tommy. Nathan, are you starting to feel better?"

To be honest, I'm not. My face is throbbing, and I can barely open my eye, yet I want Mom to walk away so I can warn Tommy about the lemonade. "I feel okay."

"Good," Mom says, taking the ice pack back. "Why don't you go change your shirt then, it has blood all over it."

I look down and smile. At least one thing was going my way today.

Chapter 3

Mom has been packing for Abby and me for weeks now. Yes, that's right, Tommy isn't the only one joining me at overnight camp. Abby is going too, and she is not happy about it. For some reason, she thought she was just going to be able to hang out at our house all summer. I'm not sure what she was planning on doing here, but I think it had something to do with boys.

Once Abby found out she was signed up for camp, she started complaining that her entire summer was ruined, and that she would be stuck in the middle of nowhere. I don't get it. Won't there be boys at Camp Spring Ridge? I mean Tommy and I will be there. Surely there must be more than just the two of us!

As predicted, on the day we leave for camp, I still have my black eye. Not only that, but my nose is still pretty swollen too. On the plus side, I can now open my eye all the way again.

Tommy's parents are not able to make the trip, so he will be riding with us. Originally, Mom and Dad were going to each drive their own cars. That way, Mom could come see us off to camp, stay with Dad a few days at his new place, and then drive back to be with Grandma. Plus, Mom was convinced we couldn't fit all of our stuff in just one car since Dad would have his things too. It was a perfect plan. Tommy and I would drive with Dad in his car, and Abby would be with Mom.

But as it turned out, the college where Dad is teaching offered to ship all of his things there ahead of time. So instead, Mom decided Dad could keep her minivan for the summer. That way we could all drive together. She would take the train back.

The minivan has plenty of room for everything as long as Dad folds down the back seats. That means Abby, Tommy, and I have to all sit together in the center row. Guess who is stuck in the middle?

Whatever. Nothing is going to ruin my good mood today. Not even the fact that I have to sit in the car for four hours with Abby while we drive to the mountains, or that she is once again in one of her *moods*. It isn't my fault Emma's parents wouldn't let her go to overnight camp. The fact remains— starting today I have six weeks of good meals coming to me! Not to mention, I still need to come up with a story to explain my bruises. A four-hour ride should do the trick.

"Mom, can we stop soon? I need to stretch."

"Abby," Mom says, turning around in her seat. "We've only been in the car twenty minutes. We've got a long way to go. We'll stop at around 11:00."

"11:00?! But that's over an hour from now! My legs are all cramped from Nathan kicking me."

"I'm not kicking you!" I say, while secretly wishing I actually could kick her and get away with it. "I'm just sitting here."

"But you are in my *space*," Abby complains.

"I am not! I'm in my own space."

"That's enough!" Mom yells. "You two need to knock it off right now. I am *not* going to listen to this bickering for another three and a half hours."

"Fine," Abby mumbles, as she slouches into her seat, elbowing me along the way. She pulls out her cell phone and begins texting. I don't know what she is complaining about. She has the next three and a half hours to sit there and do her favorite thing: text. That is all she would be doing at home anyway, except in the car, Mom isn't bugging her to put her phone away. She should be happy.

I peek over to her phone, expecting to see a conversation with Emma, but instead Abby is texting someone by the name of Niles Malloy. From the bits of the conversation I can see, it looks as though Abby might actually have a boyfriend. No wonder she doesn't want to go to camp. I wonder if Mom and Dad know about this Niles.

Tommy and I spend the next hour playing different variations of "the license plate" game. First, we try to call out different states, but after we get through Pennsylvania, New York, New Jersey, and Delaware, the variety of different plates slow down quite a bit. We then move on to calling out the alphabet in order as we see them on different license plates. When we get to z, we start over, only this time with numbers. We are up to 73, when it is finally time to stop and stretch. Because it is nearly 11:30, Mom decides we should find somewhere where we can also eat lunch. Dad turns off the highway and follows the signs to some random diner.

"Finally," Abby snaps, as she jumps out of the car, acting as if she were the only one sitting for the past hour and a half.

Inside the restaurant, we see a sign that says, "Please Wait To Be Seated," although the restaurant is practically empty. A woman and a young boy are sitting at one table, and at a second table sit two men. They have on identical blue jackets. They sort of look like the FBI guys I sometimes see in movies. I wonder. Other than that, the place is empty. There is a waitress at the counter, not doing much of anything. She finally walks up to us.

"Five for lunch?" she asks, barely looking at us.

"Yes," Mom replies.

We follow the waitress as she leads us to a large semi-circle shaped booth. Abby slides in first, followed by Mom, Dad, and Tommy. I slide in last. The waitress hands Abby, Mom, and Dad menus and places paper placemats and crayons in front of Tommy and me.

"The children's menu is on the back along with some games," the waitress says, as she motions to the placemats.

Really? Going into fifth grade and she thinks Tommy and I are only interested in a grilled cheese sandwich in the shape of a boat? Not to mention the fact that I am so hungry I feel like I could eat five burgers. Mom had decided to make scrambled eggs and sausage for breakfast. Let's just say it wasn't pretty and leave it at that. Tommy nudges me, as she walks away.

"Dad, can we look at your menu when you're done?"

"Here." Dad hands us the menu, "I'll share with Mom."

Tommy and I quickly each decide on the double cheeseburger with onion rings. Mom even agrees to let us have a soda.

As we sit and wait, there is nothing to do. A picture of a woman wearing a very large diamond ring stares back at me from the placemat. The writing under her face says, "Bring out the sparkle in her eyes," with a picture of the jewelry store that apparently promises this magic. I never really understood why diner placemats had advertisements on them. Aren't they just going to get covered in splattered food anyway?

Tommy and I take turns playing tic-tac-toe on the back of the placemat, while Mom and Dad talk about their summer schedule. Abby, of course, continues just to sit and text. You would think she'd be bored of that already, especially since she was the one so anxious to get out of the car and do something different. I wonder what Abby is going to do all summer without her phone? The camp has a strict no cell phone policy, so Abby will be handing it over to Mom once we get there. Oh boy, was Abby steamed when Mom told her about that rule!

"Do you see that?" Mom asks Dad, pointing to the table where the woman and child had been sitting.

I look to where Mom is pointing and see only the young boy, maybe five years old, sitting all by himself at a table. The two guys who had been sitting at the only other occupied table had already left.

"I can't believe a parent would just leave a little kid sitting alone like that. That's a disgrace. Something could happen to that poor kid. You read about kids missing in the paper everyday."

The boy doesn't seem to mind. He is sitting at the table playing with a handheld video game. I don't see what the big deal is. In fact, I wish I had thought of bringing my own. It's not that I don't want to hang out with Tommy for a four-hour drive, but having a video game to play along the way would certainly help the time pass. I mean, there are just so many rounds of the license plate game a kid can play.

A tall kid, maybe about eighteen or so, walks up to the little boy and starts talking to him. Must be his brother, I think. The little boy ignores him and continues to play his game. Suddenly, the teenager reaches down and tries to pull the game out of the boy's hand.

"Hey!" the boy yells, not letting go. "That's mine!"

"Give it up, kid," the teenager says, still trying to pull the game out of the little kid's hands. The boy will not let go.

The teenager grabs the kid by his arm and tries to yank him completely out of his chair. "Didn't you hear me, kid? I said I want that game," he angrily says.

"Help!" the boy yells. "Somebody help!"

I race out of my seat and run up to the teen. I pull

the little boy from his grasp. The boy falls to the ground, but his video game is in the teen's hands.

"Nate Rocks! Thank goodness you're here!" the little boy yells, hugging my leg as I face the teen.

"Leave him alone!" I shout to the teen, as I help the boy up.

"Oh yeah? Who's gonna make me? You?" the teen starts laughing.

I look behind me hoping that Tommy and possibly even Dad are on their way to help me, but I am all alone. Come to think of it, they are no longer even sitting in the booth. I reach into the blue jacket I am suddenly wearing and pull out an ID held in a black leather case.

"FBI, son. Now let go of the video game."

The teen stares at my badge, drops the game on the table, and tries to run, but the chairs have him locked in. I reach into the other pocket of my jacket and pull out a pair of shiny handcuffs. I try to grab the teen's arm, but he pulls it out of reach too quickly. The little boy runs out of the restaurant. The teen lifts one of the chairs and swings it at me, clipping me in the eye. Pain rushes through my head, but I shake it off. He swipes the video game off the table, but I knock it out of his hands and onto the floor. The game smashes open as it hits the floor, and hundreds of tiny sparkling diamonds fall out of the back. I look back up at the teen as he leaps onto the table, trying to jump over the chairs to make his escape. I grab his leg, pulling him with all my might to the ground. He tries to push me off of him. We roll on the ground, each of us trying to gain control of the other until finally I manage to hold him down and secure the handcuffs tightly around his wrists.

The two men who had left earlier come running back into the restaurant with the little boy.

"Nate Rocks! I don't believe it! You've captured Niles Malloy!" FBI man number one excitedly proclaims.

"Niles Malloy?" I ask, looking down at the defeated teenager, still lying on the ground.

"Yes! Didn't you know? He is on the FBI most wanted list. He has been robbing jewelry stores all throughout the country. He steals jewels and hides them in kids' toys. Then he smuggles them out of the country where he sells them for millions of dollars. Isn't that right, Niles?"

Niles looks up at the burley FBI agent, but he only grunts before lowering his head back to the ground.

FBI man number one continues. "We've been trying to catch him for months now, but he always manages to escape. We can't thank you enough, Nate. You are a true hero."

"Hey kid," FBI man number two asks the little boy, "where did you get that game?"

The kid looks down at the ground and mumbles, "I...I...I...found it in the parking lot. I'm sorry. I shouldn't have taken it."

"It's okay, kid," FBI man number one says. "Next time, let a grownup know." FBI man number two pulls Niles up to his feet and leads him outside and into the back of a van.

FBI man number one walks over to me and points

to my eye. "That's quite a shiner you have there, Nate. Are you going to be okay?"

I touch my eye. "Oh this? It's no big deal. I'm fine."

"Well, thanks again," he says, as he walks out the door. "Oh and put some ice on that eye."

"Some what?" I ask, barely able to hear him.

"Ice! She said ice! Nathan, what is wrong with you?"

"What?" I ask, looking up at Mom.

"The waitress is asking you if you want ice in your soda. Could you stop drawing for a moment and pay attention please?"

I look down at the picture of myself with a black eye. "Uh—sorry. Sure, I'll have some ice, thanks."

Abby leans across the table to look at my picture. "He's probably just trying to think up some story to tell his new camp friends to explain the black eye," Abby sneers. "Can't go around telling them a *girl* beat you up, right, Nathan? What are you going to tell them anyway? That you got it fighting for justice? Saving the world? Rescuing a damsel in distress?"

I look over at Abby. "I'm going to tell them the truth."

Chapter 4

"You're really going to tell them Lisa hit you with a horseshoe?" Tommy asks, as we walk back toward the car.

"Not exactly," I answer.

"But inside you told Abby you were going to tell them the truth."

"I am," I say. I stop and look at Tommy. "I'm going to tell them I got it while trying to help someone. That's true. I was helping. I was helping to keep Lisa out of everyone else's hair."

"Well, what if they ask for more details?"

"I don't know. I'll just tell them I don't want to brag about it."

Tommy nods his head in approval as we get back into the van. Only three more hours to go until we reach Camp Spring Ridge.

The hours pass relatively quickly. Tommy and I try to play I spy, but since we are moving, it gets kind of hard to keep a single item in view for very long.

As we head up a winding gravel road following the signs to camp, I can't help but notice there is not much around except farms. Lots and lots of farms. Maybe Abby was right. Maybe this camp really is in the middle of nowhere. At least we won't go hungry, not with all these cornfields around.

"Darn it!" Abby complains. "I've lost my cell phone reception." She shoves the phone into her pocket and sulks further down into her seat.

"Hey! Look at that, a totem pole!" Tommy says, pointing out his window. I lean over to take a peek. Sure enough, sitting on the edge of the road is a giant totem pole. In fact, there is a second totem pole out Abby's window with a sign above it, connecting the two poles, with the words: "Camp Spring Ridge." I guess we are here.

Dad drives through the entrance. It looks as if we have entered a forest—a dark, creepy forest. The trees seem as if they are about to come alive at any second and snatch our car. I'm starting to have second thoughts about this summer camp thing. Thankfully, the forest eventually opens up into an open field filled with wooden cabins. I see in front of us, a group of people, jumping around and waving their arms at us. I think they are yelling for us to turn around and go home. You know, because of the haunted forest and all. As we get closer, however, I realize they are cheering and clapping as if we are celebrities. We drive past them and stop at a man wearing a white shirt and holding a clipboard. Dad rolls down his window as we approach him.

"Afternoon folks!" the man says, all bright and chipper sounding. He peeks into the back seat of our van at Tommy, Abby, and me. "And who do we have here?"

"Abby Rockledge, Nathan Rockledge, and Tommy

Jensen," Dad replies.

The man with the clipboard searches his list and then looks back at Dad. "Ah yes, we've been expecting you all. Now let's see where you kids are staying." He flips through some of his pages and looks back at us. "Hmmm, it seems all of our bunks are full, but I'm sure we can set up a couple of tents for you all back there in that forest you just drove through."

"In the for-for-forest?" I stammer.

"Aw, I'm just kidding with you," the man says laughing.

I, on the other hand, am not laughing. In fact, I'm pretty certain that overnight camp is now just the worst idea ever. I want to go home, even if it does mean a summer full of Mom's awful cooking and hanging around Lisa Crane.

I must look terrified because the man looks directly at me and says, "Don't worry, son, the forest is strictly off limits. Camp rules."

Trust me, that won't be a problem, I think to myself, as I nod.

"Now let's see." He flips through his papers one more time. "Abby, you are with the Sparrows on the other side of the lake."

"The Sparrows?" she asks, looking a bit worried herself.

"Oh yes, didn't you know? All of our bunks are named after birds we commonly see around camp. Your bunk is named after our Lark Sparrow, one of the most lovely and beautiful chirpers around."

Abby suddenly sits up tall in her seat as if her

bunk's bird was specifically chosen for her.

The man points to another row of trees. "Follow the path down the hill. It will lead you around the lake and into the girls' camp. The boys are on this side of camp. Let's see ...ah yes, you boys are in the Hawks, one of my personal favorites."

"Are you sure they are not with the Cuckoos?" Abby mutters under her breath.

I elbow Abby in the side as the man continues, looking at Mom, "If you want, we can load Abby's things into our camp van to take you and Abby over to the girls' camp while Dad here helps the boys."

Mom looks at Dad and shrugs her shoulders. Dad replies, "Sure, that would be great."

"Okay then. My name is Jerry Franks. I'm the camp director. It sure is nice to meet you folks. The Hawks' bunk is down this road and on the right. I'll send the van over there to collect Abby's things."

"Thanks, Jerry. Great to meet you too." Dad drives down the bumpy dirt road toward a group of wooden cabins. We look for the one with the "Welcome Hawks" banner, park, and start to unload the car.

A tall lanky kid comes out of the cabin and takes one of the duffle bags from Dad.

"Hi, I'm Matt. I'm the counselor for the Hawks."

Dad picks up a second duffle bag and motions towards Tommy and me as we stand beside him, "Hi Matt. This here is Nathan and Tommy."

"Hey guys," Matt says. "Welcome to the Hawks."

Off to the side, a group of maybe ten other boys are all hanging out, laughing, and goofing around. I wonder if they are also Hawks.

Just as we get the car unloaded, a very loud, rattling van pulls up next to us. An older woman wearing a floppy wide brimmed hat and a Camp Spring Ridge t-shirt gets out of the driver's seat. A very fat dog jumps out behind her and sits under a tree, looking quite uncomfortable. The woman attempts to close the van door several times, but it keeps swinging back open. She finally gives up, leaving the door open and walks up to where Abby and Mom are standing. The woman trips over a large tree root and nearly falls into Mom.

"Ah, you must be Abby!" the woman says.

"Yes," Abby says, looking a bit hesitant.

"I'm Claudia," Mom says, reaching her hand out, "Abby's mom."

The woman ignores Mom's hand and gives her a big hug instead. Abby steps back. I know she is hoping to escape a hug of her own, but the woman is too fast. She grabs Abby's arm and yanks her in.

Abby finally escapes. The woman straightens her hat and says, "Very nice to meet you both. I'm Tasha. I work alongside Jerry, making sure all the kids here have a great summer. You can call me *Mama T*. Over there is Daisy." She points to the tree where the dog is sitting and panting.

"Is she okay?" Mom asks.

"Daisy? Oh my, yes. She's just getting ready to have her pups. I expect it will be just another couple of weeks. Jerry told me I could find you here. Shall we load up your things, Abby?"

Abby looks over to the rusted old van with its door

practically hanging off and its engine sounding as if it is about to die at any moment.

"Uh, sure I guess," she replies, as Mama T starts tossing Abby's bags into the back of the van.

Mom walks over to me and throws her arms around my body, in front of everyone...EVERYONE.

"Oh, Nathan!" she wails, "I've never been away from you this long! I'm going to miss you so much!"

I try to break free, but her clutch is too strong. The other kids have stopped what they are doing and are now all watching us.

"Now don't forget," she continues, still using her *my voice gets louder and higher pitched whenever I get upset* voice, "make sure you write home and don't drink too much water before you go to sleep."

"Yeah, Nathan," Abby blurts just as loudly, "you know what happens when you drink to much water before bedtime. I just hope for the sake of the other Hawks that you don't get a top bunk!"

"That's not funny, Abby!" I break away and try to take a swing at her, but she jumps into the van too fast for me to get her and slides the door shut.

I look over at the other boys, who are now staring at me. Even Tommy has taken a few steps back, seemingly trying to disassociate himself from me.

"Now, Nathan," Mom continues, only this time in a low voice so no one else can hear. "You know that's not what I meant. I just know how sometimes you get the hiccups and can't fall asleep." Mom kisses the top of my head one more time and gives Tommy a normal hug. "You boys have a great time."

"Thanks, Mrs. Rockledge," Tommy replies.

"Nathan," Mom says, picking up my backpack off the ground. "There's a big hole in your bag."

Dad takes the bag out of her hands to examine it more closely. "Oh, that's no big deal, Nathan. I think I have some duct tape in the car. I'll patch it right up for you."

Mama T walks back over to us as Dad fixes my bag. "What is it about you men and your duct tape? I swear Jerry thinks he can fix just about anything with it. Are you ready?" she asks Mom.

Mom nods and turns back to me. "Well, I guess this is it," she says, thankfully sparing me the dramatics this time.

"I'll be there as soon as I get the boys settled," Dad says, as Mom gets into the van. We watch as they disappear down the dirt road.

"Hey, Nathan, did I ever tell you about the time Uncle Robert and I went to overnight camp? I was just about your age."

"You mean the time you and Uncle Robert snuck out of your bunk in the middle of the night because you and some kids from the next bunk thought it would be fun to go hiking after dark?"

"Yeah, that was a fun summer," Dad says with that familiar glazed look in his eyes. "You boys are going to have a great time!" he says, snapping back into reality. "I can't wait to hear all about it. Well, I guess I should go find Mom and Abby. Have fun!" He thankfully forgoes the dramatic hug and quickly pats Tommy and me on our backs before walking away.

I look at Tommy as Dad drives off. "What he

forgot to tell you was that they got lost hiking, were covered in poison ivy, and had to spend the rest of the week in the infirmary recovering."

Matt walks over to Tommy and me and puts his arms around our shoulders. "Come on, boys. Let me introduce you to the rest of the Hawks."

Chapter 5

We follow Matt over to the side of the cabin where the other kids are now standing. Some are talking with others, laughing, and messing around, while a few of them are just standing there, looking as lost as I feel. I'm relieved to see that Tommy and I are not the only newbies here.

"All right, Hawks, gather around," Matt says. "I think we are all here now." I look up. The sky seems to be getting slightly darker, and the wind is starting to pick up a little.

Tommy and I find a seat at the picnic table along with the other boys. Matt stands at the end, looking very official with his clipboard and whistle. Apparently clipboards are all the rage here at Camp Spring Ridge.

"Welcome Hawks. I'm Matt, your counselor. I've been coming to Camp Spring Ridge every summer since I was your age. This is a great place, and it's my job to make sure you boys have the best summer ever." Matt looks up at the sky as the wind rustles through the papers on his clipboard. "Now, before it starts raining, let's see if we can get through some of the camp rules."

"Rules? We don't need any dumb rules! It's summer!"

I look over toward the sound of the husky voice to see a boy who looks more like he's Abby's age than my age. He also appears to have arms as big as my thighs and no-neck. I've never seen anyone without a neck before. I'm sure it's there somewhere. It's just that this kid's head is enormous. I am in the right bunk aren't I?

Matt doesn't seem disturbed by the outburst as he continues right along. "The rules are only there to make sure you have the most fun possible while staying safe. We wouldn't want anyone getting hurt...or worse."

Worse?! Tommy and I look at each other. I turn around to scan the dirt road. Dad must still be at Abby's bunk. If I left right now and ran, I could probably get there before he and Mom leave. I'm sure Mom would take me with her to see Grandma once I explained about how dangerous it is here at camp. She's always saying we don't get to visit with Grandma enough. Or I could just stay at Tommy's house. I'm certain Tommy would follow me if I took off running. But what if they were already gone? Then I would have to return to my bunk. I could already hear the other kids laughing at me as the camp director returned me to the Hawks.

"Okay," Matt starts, holding down the paper on his clipboard. "Rule #1: Always listen to your counselor—he's the coolest guy here." Matt starts laughing, but quickly notices no one else joins in.

He clears his throat and continues. "Rule #2: Stay with your bunk at all times unless you have specific permission to go somewhere. Rule #3: Lights out at 10:00pm. Rule #4: When it's our turn to have kitchen duty, *everyone* must participate, and the most important rule—Rule #5: Stay out of the forest! Look, you guys are old enough to hear this, so I'm just going to tell it to you straight. The forest may look cool, but it's big and dangerous. Every summer, one or two campers decide to wander in there, and the same thing always happens. They get lost. The camp has to call in a search party with dogs and the whole bit. If you wander too far in, you might run across snakes or even coyotes and wolves. So do yourselves a favor and stay out!"

I look around the table to see everyone staring at Matt...even No-Neck.

"I know some of you have been here before, but it looks like we have a bunch of new faces." Matt picks up a plastic bag that had been by his feet and dumps out the contents onto the table. A pile of markers and white "Hello My Name is..." stickers fall out. "Everyone grab a pen and a name tag, and let's start getting to know each other."

"Oh brother," Tommy complains, as he starts writing his name.

I have to agree. Writing our names on tags is a bit corny, but there *are* a lot of kids to remember.

A wind gust catches the nametag I have in front of me before I can finish writing my name. I jump off the bench to try to grab it, but I keep missing, stumbling with every step as the nametag gets carried further and further down the dirt road. The rain is just starting to come down now, lightly hitting my face. I try to catch the nametag, but it keeps picking up speed with every gust. Without any warning, the rain comes down even heavier, quickly turning the once dirt road into a river of mud. I can see Jerry up ahead waving at me as he did when we first arrived at camp. I know, I get it: *Welcome to Camp Spring Ridge*, blah, blah, blah. So far it's been a blast.

As I get closer, however, I can see he is not smiling the way he was when we first arrived. Something is definitely wrong. I pick up my pace, trying to race through the sticky, rising muddy waters toward him.

"Nate! Thank goodness you're here! We need help!"

"Jerry, what's wrong? Where did all this water and mud come from?"

"It's coming through an opening in the fence!" Jerry exclaims, pointing across a field I hadn't noticed before. Sure enough, mud and water are pouring through the hole at an alarming rate. "We've got to fix it, or else the entire camp will be swallowed up by a muddy river! You're the only one who can save us!"

"Me? Why me?" I ask, confused.

"Why because you're Nate Rocks, of course!"

I look down and suddenly notice I am wearing thigh high yellow rubber boots over yellow rubber pants, topped with a yellow rubber raincoat. Jerry is wearing the same silly outfit as me. How does he expect me to stop the water? Wait a minute... That's it!

"Jerry, we need to plug the hole with something waterproof, something that will be strong enough to hold back the mud and water."

"But what?" Jerry asks. "We don't have time to drive around camp looking for anything, plus I don't think this old van could even get though all this mess even if we wanted her to."

Jerry motions over to the driveway next to where he is standing. The clunky old van that had picked up Mom and Abby is now parked there. Did it always have that canoe tied to its rooftop?

"Jerry, do you have any more of these rain outfits anywhere close by?"

"Actually, there are a whole bunch of boxes full of them in the van. We were about to go distribute them to all the bunks before we realized we wouldn't be able to get through."

"Perfect!" I exclaim.

"Nate, we don't have time to play dress up! The mud is almost up to our knees already!"

I look over once again to the van. Silver tape that is holding the bumper on to the body of the van catches my eye.

"Jerry, what about that tape. Is there any extra?"

"You mean *duct tape*? Oh yeah, I've got tons. Mama T is always laughing at me for having so much. I swear, you can fix anything with duct tape. Just look at how I fixed up her van. Good as new! Hold on, are you suggesting we tape up the hole? I'm not sure that is going to work, Nate."

"No, but we are going to use duct tape to seal it up once we stuff all of the rain gear in to plug up the hole. The rubber from the clothing will keep the mud from seeping through, and we'll use duct tape to hold it in place. We just have to get all the supplies across the field and over to that fence."

"I already told you, Nate, this van isn't going anywhere with the field all flooded out. There must be over two feet of mud and water across it, and it's growing by the second!"

"Not the van, Jerry. The canoe! Quick, help me untie it. We need to get across the field as quick as possible."

Jerry releases the cords that secure the canoe, and we lift it carefully, resting it on the top of the water. He pulls two oars out of the van as well as the boxes of rain gear and places them into the boat. He then reaches into the glove compartment of the van and grabs a large roll of silver tape. The rain is coming so fast now, I can barely see across the field. The water, just at my knees moments ago, is now over my hips.

"All ready!" Jerry yells above the sound of the rushing water.

We jump into the canoe, each grabbing an oar and start to row toward the hole in the fence. Seconds seem like hours as we make our way through, fighting the rain and wind. The rain feels like pellets as it hits my face, yet I keep going, knowing we are getting closer with every stroke. Finally, the tip of the canoe hits the fence. Jerry rips open the boxes and starts handing me the rubber rain gear. I stuff them through the hole, fighting the strong current of the water pushing its way through. With each item, the flow slows slightly until we have used every last article of clothing to stop the water. Jerry tears long strips of duct tape so I can cover the entire hole, keeping everything firmly in place. The area around the hole is now completely dry. Not one drop of rain or mud can be seen coming through.

I lean back to admire my handiwork.

"You did it, Nate! You did it!" Jerry yells, nearly tipping the canoe as he gets up to hug me. You saved Camp Spring Ridge!

The waters start to recede, despite the heavy rain still coming down. I can even see small specks of grass reappear in the field.

"Nathan—hey, Nathan! Come on!" I look up at Tommy who is standing next to me, dripping wet. He looks at my nametag, still on the picnic table. "You were supposed to write your name, not draw a picture of yourself in a raincoat! Anyway, it's pouring out here, and Matt wants everyone inside the cabin before it gets too muddy out. He says we were supposed to get a box of rain gear from Jerry, but it seems to have gone missing."

I look down at the tiny mud pile forming beneath my feet. *I just may know where that went*, I think to myself.

Chapter 6

Since I missed all the introductions outside, I have to rely on Tommy to help decipher the ink blotched nametags everyone is wearing. From what we can tell, we have a Jason, Danny, Mark, Charlie, Walt, Lee, and Joel. No-Neck has apparently decided he doesn't need a nametag. So be it.

While we wait for the rain to end, Matt suggests we unpack all our things. Matt lets us pick our own beds. There are several rows of bunk beds lining the walls. Tommy and I each grab our bags and walk to the back of the cabin. There is a row of shelves going up the wall directly next to the bed.

"Do you want top or bottom?" Tommy asks.

"Bottom I guess," I respond, looking up at the top bunk. I've never slept in bunk beds before. That top bunk looks awfully high to me. The last thing I needed was to fall off the bed and get even more bruises.

"Cool." Tommy throws his sleeping bag up to the top bunk and climbs right up. "I'll take the top three shelves, and you can have the bottom three."

I unzip the first duffle bag and start unpacking my things.

"So what happened to you?" a voice next to me says.

Unsure if this kid is talking to me, I turn around and ask, "Me?"

"Yeah, your eye. What happened?"

I scan the boy's shirt to read his nametag: Joel.

"Oh," I say, bringing my hand up. I knew the question would come eventually. I wish I had thought of an actual story to tell. Instead I go with my original plan. "I was helping someone and got hit."

Out of nowhere, No-Neck appears right in my face, examining my eye.

"I'll bet a girl slugged him," he says, smirking. "What'd you do, squirt, try to steal her Barbies?"

"Yeah, what's the real story?" another kid says, walking up to me. His nametag is all smeared, but I can see it starts with an M and only has four letters. This must be Mark.

"Well ...um," I begin.

"It's true."

I turn back around to see that Tommy has climbed off his top bunk and is now standing next to me.

"Nathan here was just trying to help someone. He got a little too close to the action and got slugged. I'm not surprised really. Nathan is always trying to help people. Did you know he saved the lives of two people who were drowning in the Atlantic Ocean last winter?"

"Really?" another boy asks. This time, I can see the nametag clearly: Charlie.

"Yup," Tommy continues, "I saw it with my

own eyes. These two teenagers were screaming for help, and there was no lifeguard on duty at the beach. Without even hesitating, Nathan grabbed the lifesaver and rope off the lifeguard chair and ran right into the water. He completely ignored the black flag warnings that said 'no swimming' just to save their lives. The waves were so rough that poor Nathan almost got swept away by the waves himself. But he was determined and pulled the two people ashore to safety."

The remaining kids are huddled around listening to Tommy and staring at me. I just know my face must be bright red with embarrassment. Still, I'm grateful that Tommy turned the conversation away from my eye.

"Aw, big deal," No-Neck says, throwing his arms up in the air. He walks back over to his bunk, which is thankfully several beds away and shoves his clothes into the shelves.

"Okay guys," Matt yells, appearing out of nowhere. "Now that you're settled in, let's get down to business."

The kids quickly forget about me and my heroics and head on over to where Matt is standing. As soon as they are out of earshot, I lean into Tommy and whisper, "Thanks."

Tommy just smiles at me and joins the group. I follow along.

"Hawks," Matt begins, as we all stand around him in a big cluster. "It's now 4:00p.m. Dinner begins at 5:00p.m., and we have kitchen duty today. That means we have to help the cafeteria staff serve and clean up."

As if we had been practicing for weeks, all ten of us groan in unison.

"Now, now, let's not complain. Every bunk has to help. It's not that bad. Dinner is much better then breakfast. The cookies they serve at dinner are pretty good. We might even be able to snag some of the leftovers for later, but you didn't hear that from me." Matt winks at us. To be honest, the thought of some extra homemade cookies is a bit tempting.

Charlie, who had been standing next to me the whole time and apparently was here last summer, must have been reading my mind because he leans over and whispers in my ear, "Don't get too excited, they taste like bakery rejects."

That may be true, but they can't possibly be worse than Mom's cookies. I'd much rather eat bakery rejects over cardboard any day.

Once we arrive at the dining hall, we are introduced to a skinny, bald man named Luke. Luke is in charge of feeding all us campers, and from what I can tell; he does not enjoy his job very much. He skips over the friendly greeting and immediately puts us to work, splitting us into small groups. Tommy, Charlie, and I are put together. Our first task is to make sure there are four full pitchers on every table: one each of milk, water, apple juice, and fruit punch. Charlie has already warned me to stay away from the fruit punch. I decide that Charlie is someone I need to become friends with.

After we are finished with drinks, we need to

make sure each table has a stack of cups, napkins, and all utensils. I feel like I'm still at home and begin to wonder if maybe Mom is sending me to camp just to have me brush up on my chores. I suppose it could be worse, the other Hawks are back in the kitchen helping with the cooking and meal preparation. From what I can tell, it smells like we are having hamburgers today. I'm okay with that. In fact, I'm pretty much looking forward to anything cooked by someone other than Mom.

When we are done getting all of the tables set up, it's time for us to get ready to help serve. Everything is set behind a long cafeteria counter. I was right. We are having hamburgers, along with French fries, corn, and salad. There is also a sandwich station where you can have something made up for you if you don't like the hot meal of the day. Looks like Tommy, Charlie, and I are making the sandwiches today.

At exactly 5:00p.m., Luke walks to the entrance of the dining hall and rings a large bell that is hanging on the wall. Within seconds, kids start piling in, lining up to order their food. Because we are serving, we have to wait until everyone else is seated before we can eat. I wish I had known this ahead of time. I am starving. I wonder if they'll notice a missing piece of cheese here and there in between making sandwiches. I happen to be very good at sneaking food.

Making sandwiches turns out to be a breeze. The choices are peanut butter and jelly, turkey, ham, roast beef, and cheese. I guess we are doing a pretty good job because no one has complained so far. I never realized how easy sandwich making actually is. Maybe Mom will let me take over cooking duty when I get home from camp. I'll score double points by saving her work, plus I'll be guaranteed to get a decent meal. Why didn't I think of this before?

"I'll have a peanut butter and jelly on wheat."

I look up to see Abby. It's the first time I've seen her since she rode off in Mama T's van earlier.

"Hey, Abby. How's it going?"

Abby turns to the girl standing next to her and says, "This is my little brother, Nathan."

"Hi," I say, waiting to be introduced to the girl, but they both just continue to look at me.

After a strange and silent staring match, Abby finally says, "So...peanut butter and jelly on wheat?"

"Oh, sure." I start to spread peanut butter on the bread, wondering what Abby is up to.

"No, Nathan!" Abby yells. "You know I don't like crunchy. Don't you have creamy peanut butter?"

What? How would I know that? I don't even remember ever seeing Abby eat peanut butter. Tommy and Charlie stop making sandwiches; everyone in line is now looking at us.

"Um, I don't see any," I respond, completely confused.

"Well, then I want roast beef with cheese and mayo on a roll."

"Okay," I say, tossing the bread with the peanut butter in the trash.

I pick up the mayo and am about to squirt it out when Abby squeals, "No, Nathan! I said mustard!

Can't you do anything right?"

"Sorry," I say, gritting my teeth. I pick up the mustard bottle and tilt it toward the roll.

I spread out the mustard, add the cheese, and pick up a couple of slices of roast beef.

"No, no, no! That roast beef is way too fatty. Give me turkey instead."

I put the roast beef back down and slowly place the turkey on the sandwich, waiting for Abby to protest. She manages to stay silent. I place the top of the roll onto the turkey and present her with her sandwich. She grabs the plate out of my hand and examines it.

"This turkey smells funny. Nevermind! We'll just have hamburgers." And without so much as a thanks or goodbye, Abby turns on her heels and heads over to the hot meal line.

"I think *she* smells funny," Tommy says, as she walks away.

"Who was that?" Charlie asks.

"You don't want to know," I reply, taking a bite of her sandwich.

Chapter 7

"Mail call!" yells Matt.

Everyday, while we are at lunch, someone from the main office delivers the mail to our bunk. Mom must be really bored over at Grandma's house because she writes to me almost every day. Usually it's something uninteresting like how Grandma's vegetable garden has a new tomato or something. Tommy's mom writes to him a lot about her garden also. I wonder why it is our moms think we are so interested in vegetables? Occasionally, Tommy's mom sends a package filled with cookies or brownies. On these days, Tommy is the most popular kid in the bunk. Otherwise, it's pretty much just Tommy, Charlie, me, and another kid who wasn't here last year, Lee, hanging out. The other kids are okay, I guess. They hang out with us when they feel like it. All but No-Neck. For whatever reason, he never seems to want to be around us.

"Get anything good?" Charlie asks.

"Just the usual," Tommy says, folding the letter from his Mom back up.

I pick up the large manila envelope from my pillow and notice Dad's handwriting. So far, Dad has only written me one other time to tell me how his new next door neighbor reminded him of the person he and Uncle Robert used to work with at the movie theater when they were sixteen...as if I would even know who Dad was talking about.

I open the envelope. A book slides out with a note from Dad.

"What's that?" Lee asks.

I turn the book over and read the torn cover, which appears to have been taped back together several times: "1,001 Ways to Ward Off Ghosts."

Tommy takes the book out of my hands while I unfold the letter and read out loud:

Dear Nathan,

I found this book when I was packing to come out here and forgot to give it to you. Uncle Robert and I brought it with us to camp when we were kids and found it quite useful. Hope you are having fun. Miss you!

Love,
Dad

"A book on how to get rid of ghosts? Do you think he's serious?" Charlie asks, taking the book out of Tommy's hands.

"Nah," Tommy replies laughing. "Nathan's Dad is always joking around. Isn't that right, Nathan?"

"Uh yeah," I say, tossing the letter back onto my pillow. I'm glad Tommy is so sure because, I have to be honest, I'm not entirely convinced.

"Besides, he didn't even go to this camp. How would he know if there were any ghosts here," Tommy continues, trying to convince Lee and Charlie who are now just staring at us, looking a bit freaked out and, in turn, are now freaking me out as well.

"Okay, Hawks," Matt says, "a little change in schedule. We'll do our letter writing tonight before bed. At the moment, we've been challenged to a kickball game against the Ravens."

Kickball? I hate kickball! It's bad enough I have to play kickball at school! You mean I have to play kickball at camp too? I thought summer camp was supposed to be fun.

Apparently, I'm the only one who feels this way, for the other kids go tearing out of the cabin, nearly knocking Matt over.

"Come on, Nathan, it will be fun," Matt says.

"Okay, I'll be right there." I stuff Dad's letter into my back pocket and head out the door, following Matt to the fields.

At least we don't have to pick teams since it's our bunk against the other bunk. I don't think I could stand being the last one picked on a team at school *and* at camp. Plus, it shouldn't be too bad—after all, the Ravens are a whole year younger than us.

The Ravens are already in the field waiting for us to start by the time Matt and I make it over to them. If you ask me, I think some of those kids must have been held back because they surely don't look like the kids from my school who just finished up third grade. At least we have No-Neck on our side.

Matt lines us up to get ready to kick. Somehow, I am placed fourth in line. At school, I'm always last. Danny, Jason, and Walt all go before me. They each kick the ball down the middle and wind up on base. The Ravens may be big, but evidently they can't catch or throw for beans. Maybe this will go okay after all.

I walk over to the plate. With bases loaded, there's no doubt in my mind I'm going to bring in a run. If I kick the ball hard enough, I may even bring in all four runs. I'd love to see the look on the kids' faces back at school when Tommy tells them about my killer kick. You can bet I'd no longer be the last one picked on the team. Shoot, they'd probably have to flip a coin just to see who gets to pick me first.

The Raven's counselor rolls the ball toward me. Instead of waiting for it to get to me, I decide to get a running start. I pull back my leg as I see the ball approaching. I need to swing it back forward at just the right second to get the perfect kick. Ready... and....NOW! I kick my leg as hard as I can. I can feel the ball catch the toe of my foot as my entire body flies up before crashing back down onto the grass, face down.

"Ow," I say softly, then..."OW!" Not so softly.

Tommy, Matt, and the counselor for the Ravens all run to me.

"Nathan! Nathan! Are you okay?" Matt yells, putting his face right into mine as if he is checking to see if I'm breathing.

"I think so," I say, pushing myself up to sitting, partially to see if I can and partially so Matt will back up a little.

"Well, why don't we have the nurse check you over just to be sure," Matt says, helping me up to my feet. Admittedly, the ground feels a bit shaky.

"I'll take him," Tommy volunteers.

Tommy grabs hold of my elbow and helps me walk off the field. As we walk past the kids in my bunk, I hear No-Neck mumble, "Nice work, twinkle toes."

"Don't worry about him," Tommy says, as we walk over to the wooden building housing the nursing station, "he has about as much grace as an elephant."

"Yeah," I say, chuckling and feeling better already.

We walk through the doorway to find a room filled with kids lying on cots. A woman wearing a white nurse's jacket sees me limping and has me sit down in the empty chair next to her desk.

"Football?" she asks.

"No, kickball," I answer.

"Ah, kickball will do it every time. I'm Nurse Patty." Nurse Patty bends my leg back and forth. "Does that hurt?" she asks.

"Yes," I wince. What I really wanted to say was, "Of course that hurts! Isn't that why I'm here? Doesn't the blood gushing indicate that I might be in pain?"

"Well, I don't think anything is broken. Let's get that cleaned up. We'll have you put some ice on it for a little bit." She looks up at Tommy and says, "You can go back to your bunk, I'm sure your friend here will be able to join you in no time."

"Okay," says Tommy. "Feel better, Nathan."

"Thanks," I say as I take my place on the only

empty cot left.

I watch as Nurse Patti cleans up my knee. Once all the blood is cleaned up I can see there are two round scrapes on my kneecap. They sort of look like a snakebite.

"Those sharp pebbles leave nasty cuts," Nurse Patty says as she pats my knee dry. "You're lucky you only have two little cuts. I've seen a lot worse than this. Here's some ice. You should be good to head back in twenty minutes or so."

"Thanks."

Nurse Patty sits back at her desk. The kid in the cot next to me is asleep. Great, twenty minutes with nothing to do. I pull out the letter Dad wrote to me. I guess now would be as good a time as any to write back to him. I grab the pencil off the table next to me and start writing on the back of his letter:

Dear Dad,

Thanks for the letter and the book. I'm sitting in the nurse's office. I hurt my knee playing kickball was bit by a snake. I'm okay. I'm looking forward to visiting day. I'll write soon.

Love,
Nathan

P.S. Can you tell me which of the 1,001 ways you most recommend?

"You ready, Nathan?" Nurse Patty is standing over me with a bandage. "I'm just going to put this over your knee to keep the dirt out, and then you can head on back."

"Okay," I say and put the letter back into my pocket.

The kickball field is empty by the time I get back over there. I have no idea where the other kids from my bunk actually might be. I see a group of kids over by the edge of the lake. They look about my age, but I'm too far away to recognize anyone. I start heading in that direction, just to be sure. The grass and weeds past the edge of the field are close to knee high, making walking a bit difficult. I look around for a path, but I do not see anywhere better to walk. I manage to find a long stick and use that to push aside some of the weeds. Just as I near the lake, I notice that most of these kids are not from my bunk. They are packing up and walking off towards another field around the other side of the lake. Darn it. The thought of having to trudge all the way back through the tall grass makes my knee hurt even more.

Suddenly, a teenage boy about the same age as Matt comes running toward me.

"Nate!" he yells, "Nate! Come quick!"

What? Did I miss supper? Is that why he is calling for me? Maybe Matt sent him over to find me.

I use my stick and stumble through the grasses towards him.

"What's up?" I ask when we are finally face to face.

"We need you! One of my junior campers is in

danger. You're the only one who can save him."

I follow the counselor as quickly as I can, when all of a sudden I hear a quiet whimper. Up ahead, I see a young boy frozen, staring at the ground. He slowly looks up at me, his eyes full of fright.

"What's the matter?" I say, making my way over to him.

"Don't move!" the counselor says softly but firmly.

I stop walking. Suddenly there is another noise. It sounds like a baby's rattle shaking.

I look down to see a light brown and copper pattern moving slowly in the grass toward the young boy, the rattle from its tail sounding louder and louder. The enormous snake stops just a foot from the boy, sliding its tongue in and out in a rhythmic motion.

The counselor moves to my side and whispers in my ear, "Please, Nate, you've got to do something. We don't have much time!"

I look back at the counselor. "Me? I don't know anything about snakes! Why me?"

"Why because you're Nate Rocks, of course. Now hurry!" the counselor replies.

Think, Nate, think! Maybe I could find a rock and smash the snake. No, I probably won't be able to get close enough to its head. What if I throw a rock to make a noise? Will the snake take off thinking there is prey over by the sound? No, I remember reading somewhere that noises scare snakes. A noise might make it bite the boy. I twirl my makeshift walking stick in my hand a few times while I think. My stick! That's it! It's risky, but I have no choice. I need to get the snake perfectly, or my plan won't work, and we could all be in danger.

I lean back over to the counselor and whisper, "Back up."

The counselor quietly takes a few steps back. I wish I could have the boy step back also, but I don't want to risk any sudden movements in front of the snake.

I look at the boy and wait for him to make eye contact with me. I put my finger up to my mouth to make the "sh" sign. He nods.

I take a deep breath. Carefully and swiftly, I slide the stick under the snake, lifting it before it has a chance to slither away. Another deep breath, this time holding the air in, and with all my strength, I hurl the snake into the lake. I let my breath out in relief as I hear the splash far into the middle of the water.

Sobbing, the little boy runs to me and hugs my legs.

"You did it, Nate, you did it!" the counselor yells, picking the boy up and giving him a hug. "You are our hero!"

"Thank you, Nate! Thank you!"

"Nathan, why are you drawing pictures of snakes all over your Dad's letter?"

I look up to see Tommy standing over my cot in the nurse's office.

"What?" I ask, looking from Tommy to my paper.

"Nevermind. Matt sent me over to see if you want

to go swimming in the lake with us," Tommy explains.

"The lake?" I ask. "Um, no thanks, I think I'll sit this one out."

Chapter 8

The Fourth of July is a big deal here at Camp Spring Ridge. While most people will be relaxing and celebrating independence, not to mention the end of "the Revolution," we will be celebrating the start of a new revolution—namely Color War. Apparently, Color War is an annual tradition here at Camp Spring Ridge. Matt keeps talking about how much fun it is going to be. To be honest, I think I'd rather have a week of kitchen duty. The whole idea of Color War does not sound fun to me one bit.

During Color War, the camp is split up into three teams: red, white, and blue. After we get our team assignment, we then leave our usual bunks during the day to join our color war team. From what Charlie has told me, we spend the first day learning songs and cheers and picking our events. We spend the next day practicing, and the third day, July 4, is when we actually compete. At night there is a big Independence Day celebration by the lake with a big bonfire, talent show, and some fireworks. After that, we get to go back to being the Hawks. But for now, we're waiting for Matt to return from his staff meeting with out team assignments.

I'm kind of hoping I'm red so I can wear my red

Phillies shirt. That always gives me a little extra luck. I don't think I even have any white shirts with me. You would think they'd let you know what team you are ahead of time so you could pack appropriately. I look over to Tommy's stuff and wonder if he's got a shirt in every color.

"Okay, Hawks!" Matt yells, as he walks through the door of our cabin. "Guess what I've got?" He's holding up an envelope and has a silly grin on his face. "Your official Color War teams. Before we begin, we have to go over a couple of things: One: no trading teams. Two: I expect everyone to have good sportsmanship, and three: listen to your team captain at all times. Now let's get right to it. On the blue team, we have: Lee, Joel, and Mark."

Matt pauses as if we are all going to start cheering, but instead, all that can be heard is a small groan coming from Lee. I kind of feel bad for him since I know he doesn't really get along with Mark. I know he was hoping to stick with Tommy, Charlie, and me. Matt looks up as the three boys move off to the side and then gets back to his paper. "Now the red team."

A thought suddenly occurs to me: what if Tommy, Charlie, and I aren't on the same team? Even worse, what if Tommy and Charlie get to be together, and I'm stuck with No-Neck? Color War could potentially be *the* worst experience of my entire life!

"Awesome!" Tommy suddenly says, jabbing me in the side.

I snap out of my mini-panic attack to see Jason,

Danny, and Walt all moving to stand next to each other. Apparently they are the red team. That leaves me, Tommy, and Charlie...and No-Neck on the white team. No lucky Phillies shirt, and I have to be with No-Neck? At least I have Tommy and Charlie with me.

"On to the important stuff," Matt continues, chuckling the way he does when he tells a joke no one else ever seems to get. "Team captains: red team you're spending the next few days with Aaron, counselor for the Larks. Blue, you're with Chris, counselor for the Orioles, and white team, you get to stay with me. Now let's head out to the main fields to meet with your teams. See you all back here for lights out."

There are about thirty-five kids standing around for the white team, girls and boys. As far as I can tell, Abby is not one of them. I'm not quite sure yet if having her on a different team is a good thing or bad thing, but for now, I'm going with good.

As it turns out, Abby's team assignment doesn't actually matter. The girls and the boys are separated into sub teams: Girls White, Boys White, Girls Red, Boys Red, Girls Blue, and Boys Blue—making up a total of six teams that compete against each other. Our team, Boys White, has sixteen kids, with Matt and two other counselors as our trusty leaders.

"W-and-H-and-I-and-T-and-E spells WHITE, W-and-H-and-I-and-T-and-E spells WHITE..."

I look around at the group of boys on my team just staring at Matt as he prances around clapping his hands at every "and," chanting this mantra at the top of his lungs. Even the other two counselors are looking at him, although they do eventually join in.

"Come on guys, let's make some noise," Matt yells, not missing a beat, "W-and-H-and-I-and-T-and-E spells WHITE, W-and-H-and-I-and-T-and-E spells WHITE, W-and-H-and-I ...okay let's start with something else," Matt says, finally realizing that we have about as much S-P-I-R-I-T as a pack of slugs.

He sits down in the grass as we all form a semi-circle around him. "How about we go over the events instead? We'll have plenty of time to practice some cheers later." He flips through the pages on his clipboard. One of these days, I plan to get my hands on that clipboard to see exactly what it is that Matt keeps flipping through, especially when he always seems to land on the same page.

"Let's hope kickball isn't on the list," No-Neck snickers, looking directly at me.

Matt looks up briefly at No-Neck and then goes back to his clipboard. I'm pretty sure Matt is sick of No-Neck already, and it's only the second week of camp.

"It looks like we've got a total of fifteen events: tug-of-war, scavenger hunt, football toss, dodge ball, relay races, archery, soccer, limbo, basketball, a dance off, water polo, volleyball, a talent show, cheering, and," Matt darts a quick glance toward me, "kickball."

Ugh. Is he serious? I don't want to participate in any of those events. Can't Charlie, Tommy, and I just sit on a boat on the lake and fish while everyone else is throwing around footballs and shooting arrows? Better yet, I really need to read some more of the book Dad sent me. So far, I'm only up to way 37 of the 1,001 ways to ward of ghosts, and I'm not feeling too confident. I thought camp was supposed to be fun.

"Okay, so the deal is," Matt continues, "everyone has to participate in cheering and in the talent show."

A collective sigh escapes all of our mouths.

"After that, we can decide what events you'll all participate in, and you'll probably have to do two or three each. The scavenger hunt usually takes up the entire day, so you wouldn't be able to do any of the remaining events, except the mandatory ones."

I immediately raise my hand. "Matt!" I call, practically jumping up and down. When he looks over at me, I yell out, "I'll take scavenger hunt." I've never done a scavenger hunt before, and I'm not exactly sure what it even involves, but if it means I don't have to deal with most of those other events, I'm in!

Tommy looks at me kind of annoyed and raises his hand as well, "I'll do scavenger hunt too," he says, reluctantly.

Charlie then speaks up without raising his hand, "Can I do it also?"

"Okay," Matt says, "scavenger hunt is full. Let's move on."

While Matt continues to go through the list, assigning events to everyone else, Mama T's rackety old van rumbles up the path. She screeches her brakes to a halt and waves to us as she steps out and tries to get her sliding door to open.

"Hi, y'all," she says, sounding flustered as she carries two big plastic bags towards us. Daisy follows, looking as fat and uncomfortable as ever. I wonder when those puppies are finally going to arrive.

"Hi, Mama T," we all unenthusiastically say together.

Looking disappointed, she asks, "What kind of a welcome is that?"

"Hi, Mama T," we say once more with only a tiny increase in energy.

"Well, that's a little better." She drops the two bags to the ground. "Gang, it's time for my favorite part of Color War." She opens one of the bags and starts unloading bottles of paint, brushes, and art supplies. "T-shirts!"

She dumps the other bag into the grass. A pile of plain white shirts falls to the ground. Well at least I have something to wear now.

"I'm guessing by the look on your faces, Matt didn't explain this part yet."

Matt flips through more clipboard pages and shakes his head no.

"Well, every year, we make team shirts to wear during Color War. Not only is it a fun activity, but also it is actually your first event. The team that comes up with the best overall design gets twenty points. You've got all of the supplies you need right here. Have fun and be creative. The winner will be announced at the end of Color War."

She waves one more time before walking back

over to her van. We watch as she struggles to get her driver's door open. She helps Daisy get in and then scoots in herself. After several attempts to start the van, a puff of black smoke comes out of the back, and she drives away.

No-Neck picks up one of the shirts and pulls it over the t-shirt he is already wearing. He grabs a basketball and starts to walk toward the basketball court.

"We are you going?" Matt asks.

"We're the white team aren't we?" No-Neck asks, staring directly at Matt.

"Yes," Matt replies.

"Well, then here's my shirt." He swirls his hand around the front of his shirt as if he were showing off some sort of game show prize. "Can't get any whiter than this! Besides, I'd rather practice for my basketball event then make a lame t-shirt. It's worth a lot more than 20 points."

"Fine," Matt says, and then mumbles just loud enough for me to make out, "whatever."

A bunch of other kids decide they like No-Neck's idea and start to pick up shirts to put on also. I can tell Matt is really becoming irritated with everyone, and the other two counselors have not yet said one word to show they are also in charge.

"I'll tell you what, team," Matt begins, bagging back up what's left of the pile of shirts and art supplies. "It's almost time for our lunch break and free swim. How about we take a break and meet back up at 2:00 to work some more. If we get the shirts done quickly right after swim, we'll have plenty of time to practice our games before we wrap up for the day. Nathan, Tommy, and Charlie, since there is really nothing to practice for scavenger hunt, you guys can practice with us. You can pretend to be the other team or something. It'll be fun."

I make a mental note to work slowly on my t-shirt.

Chapter 9

Normally I look forward to the Fourth of July. Tommy's parents always have us over for burgers, and then we all walk over to the town center to watch the fireworks after the sun goes down. Abby usually spends the day over at her best friend Emma's house, which makes the day even better for me. This year we are missing all of that. Instead, we have this Color War stuff.

I manage to survive t-shirt making and the rest of day one without too much trauma. Yesterday (aka day two) wasn't that bad either. Since Charlie, Tommy, and I are doing the scavenger hunt, we really weren't needed at practice, so Matt put us in charge of making the props and scenery for the skit we are putting on tonight at the bonfire.

Matt wrote the skit, and of course, he thinks it's the funniest thing ever. If you ask me, it's kind of dumb. Each of us must wear a baseball cap, with the rim on the right side of our heads. One person is on stage sitting on a bench. One by one, each kid walks on stage and sits on the bench. The kid who is already sitting asks, "Is it time yet?" to the new person who just walked on stage, who then answers, "Nope." This routine continues until all but one of us are on stage and sitting on the bench.

When the last person finally sits, the kid next to him asks, "Is it time yet?"

The last person replies, "Yes, it's time." We all then slide out baseball caps over, so the rim is on the left side and then walk off the stage.

Apparently, everyone will think this is a riot. I don't really get it. I also don't get why it needs stage props other than a couple of benches, which we can borrow from the picnic area. Matt, however, insisted we needed to make it look like a park or a bus stop or something, so Charlie, Tommy, and I spent the day yesterday painting large cardboard trees to go around the benches.

Now that we have reached the day we have been preparing for, Matt is fully focused on one thing and one thing only: winning Color War. He is so pumped up; I'm half expecting him to have us march into the opening ceremonies wearing tribal face paint while carrying spears. Thankfully, he only wants us to wear the team t-shirts we made. Even so, his enthusiasm level is way too high for first thing in the morning.

"W-and-H-and-I-and-T-and-E spells White!" Matt yells over and over as we march single-file over to the main fields. As usual, Matt is the only one cheering. The rest of us are just sort of mumbling. We meet up with the girls of the white team. They seem to be just as enthusiastic as Matt as they join in on his cheer. They are standing in a group and holding up a banner painted in big letters on a sheet that says, "GIRLS WHITE WILL WIN THE FIGHT

TONIGHT." They also have matching t-shirts with the same words on the front and back, unlike our shirts, which just say: "Go White."

The other teams gather around and are also yelling their cheers. The screaming begins to sound like one big loud buzz. Nobody can hear what anyone else is yelling. Jerry gets on the makeshift stage and tries to yell over the noise, but really no one is paying any attention. He finally sticks two fingers into his mouth and whistles so loudly that the entire camp stops mid cheer and just stares at him.

"Ah, that's better," he says, looking quite proud of himself, although I don't know why he didn't think of using his piercing whistle five minutes ago.

"Welcome to the 45th annual Camp Spring Ridge COLOR WAR!"

Everyone goes nuts again. Even Tommy and Charlie are jumping up and down cheering. Jerry waves his arms in the air to calm us down, and we all get quiet again.

"Mama T, do we have the leaderboard ready?"

Mama T carries a huge poster board on the stage and places it on an easel that is already set up. There are six columns on the board, one for each team. Running down the side of the board is a listing of every event and how many points each event is worth. I quickly scan the board to find the scavenger hunt. 50 points for first place? It's worth at least double of every other event! Here I was hoping for a low key, no stress day.

Jerry continues once Mama T steps to the side,

"Okay kids. Your team captains have the schedule and location for each of the events. Make sure you follow all the rules or your team will be disqualified from that competition. Remember, we are here to have fun! Now go make some noise!"

Every team starts cheering one more time and then forms large huddles around its team captain.

"This is it team," Matt says, flipping through the papers on his clipboard, as usual. "Let's get our scavenger hunt guys on their way first." He unclips three sheets of paper from his board and hands them to Tommy, Charlie, and me, along with a white trash bag and three pencils that he pulls from his backpack. "Now listen up, boys." Matt leans in close to us even though we could hear him just fine from where we were standing. "This event is worth 50 points. Work quickly and whatever you do, don't get disqualified. Now go."

Charlie, Tommy, and I take off running even though we have absolutely no idea what we are looking for, or where we are going. When we get to the other side of the field, Tommy yells, "Guys, stop! STOP!"

We stop in our tracks and double over, each of us trying to catch his breath.

Tommy starts reading from the paper:

Scavenger Hunt Rules:

You have until 4:00 this afternoon to complete this list.
-You must take a mandatory break from 1:00

until 1:30p.m. to eat lunch in the dining hall. You may not leave the dining hall until 1:30p.m.

-Only three campers per team can participate in this activity.

-The forest is completely off limits.

-Items may only be taken from cabins with owner's permission and must be returned at the end of Color War.

-The team who returns with the most items by 4:00 wins.

Good Luck & here are your items:

1. A maple leaf
2. A pine cone
3. A bird feather
4. A smooth stone from the lake
5. A snake skin (please leave the snake behind)
6. A pair of dirty socks from one of the boy's counselors
7. A hairband from one of the girl's counselors
8. A harmonica
9. A four leaf clover
10. An empty water bottle

In addition —you also need to have the following counselors sign each item:

1. A counselor whose birthday it is today.
2. A counselor whose middle name is Michael.

3. *The counselor who has been here the longest.*

4. *A counselor who is here for the first time.*

5. *A counselor who is an only child.*

6. *A counselor who doesn't like chocolate.*

7. *A counselor who is allergic to dogs.*

8. *A counselor who can speak more than one language.*

9. *A counselor who is afraid of spiders.*

10. *A counselor who can stand on his or her head for 10 seconds.*

Tommy looks up at us. "Do you want to split the list up, or do you want to work together?" Tommy asks.

"Let's split up for now," Charlie suggests. "Then when we meet up for lunch we can decide if we want to work together for the rest. Does everyone have a watch so we know when to meet back up?"

We all nod.

"I'll take the first six items," I offer. They seem to involve the least interaction, plus just about all of the items can be found over by the lake. I can always get Matt to pull off his socks at the very end if I don't have time to make it back to the bunks.

"I'll take the next seven," Tommy says, "and Charlie, you get the last seven."

"Got it," Charlie says.

Tommy throws the bag at me. "Here Nathan, you take this. I'll find another bag along the way. Good luck guys. See you at 1:00."

Tommy and Charlie start walking away: Tommy towards the cabins and Charlie back towards the fields where most of the counselors are still standing. I read over my six items one more time. The snakeskin will be the most challenging, but otherwise this looks pretty simple. I should be done in no time.

There are a ton of pinecones littering the path along the lake. I pick one up, throw it in the bag, and check it off on my list. This is just too easy. I look up at each tree as I walk by, most are indeed maple trees, but the branches are just too high up for me to reach the leaves. I finally find a leaf on the ground. Check. I also quickly find a bird feather and the snakeskin that I thought was going to take me so long. I pick up each item, carefully placing them in the bag, and check them off the list. I peek back into the bag to see the snakeskin and smile to myself as I continue to the lake.

Only two items left: a smooth rock from the lake and the dirty socks. Not a problem. I see a small rowboat sitting on the edge of the water and look down at my watch. It's only 11:45. I don't have to be back until 1:00. There's nothing in the rules that says I can't take the boat out onto the lake for a little bit. The only thing forbidden in the rules is the forest. Maybe I can sit out on the water and read some more of Dad's book about warding off ghosts. I pat my back pocket to make sure the book is still there. I'm almost up to number 150, but I really want to read more....you know, in case the first 150 ways don't work.

Besides, it looks like there is already someone out on the lake. Maybe it's someone from the red or the blue team also taking a little break. Squinting, I try to focus on them, to see if I can make out the color of their dark shirt, when all of a sudden a counselor comes running towards me from the side of the lake. Was this person here the entire time? I didn't even notice.

"Nate!" she yells, "Nate! We need your help!"

"What's going on?" I ask, walking to the counselor who appears to be wearing a red team shirt. If she thinks I'm going to give up my snakeskin, she had better think again. Charlie warned me that some of the other teams might try to trick me into giving up items or helping them, but they're not going to fool me! Play it cool, Nathan, just play it cool.

"We need your help, Nate! Please!"

Oh, I bet you do, I think to myself, smirking at the counselor.

The counselor continues on with her little game. "We have to hurry! There is a shark in the water, and it won't let one of my campers back to shore! Please help!"

"A what?!" I look out to the boat. Sure enough I see a shark fin coming out of the water. It looks like it is circling the boat.

"Nate, please! You've got to save her!"

I walk over to where the small rowboat had been that was sitting at the edge of the water. It is now a high-speed powerboat.

"Stay here!" I yell, as I jump in the boat and start its powerful engines. I hold tight of the steering wheel and race off into what now appears to be a mighty ocean. The waves crash up and down from the force of the boat speeding through. My speed increases with every passing second.

I approach the small rowboat, getting closer, but not so close as to alarm the enormous great white shark. The camper, a young girl, is screaming and waving her arms at me. The shark continues its steady path, circling her boat. I silence my engine as I get closer, allowing my boat to drift toward her. What was it we learned about sharks in Mrs. Dempsey's fourth grade science class? Didn't they use their sense of smell to find their prey? I look around my boat and notice a large bucket full of slimy fish. Yes! That's it!

"Hang on!" I yell to the girl.

"Please, Nate! Help me!" she cries, her voice full of terror. "Please!"

I pull on the heavy plastic gloves that are on the floor. I look into the bucket, not happy about the fact that I need to pick one of these stinky, slippery things up. Thank goodness for the gloves. I hold my breath as I pick up one of the slimy fish. I throw it near the shark and away from the rowboat. I need to make sure the shark will go for it. Sure enough, the shark leaves its circular path and dives into the water to find the food. He is back within seconds, leaving me no time to rescue the girl, and once again begins to circle her boat.

The girl starts wailing in hysterics.

"Don't worry," I yell to her. "That was only a test!"

I start my engine up again so I will be able to move

quickly. At the same time, I pick up the bucket with both hands, and hurl the contents as far from us as possible, hoping the shark will take note. He'd better, as I'm not quite sure of what my plan B will be.

As expected, the shark leaves the circular path one more time, swimming and diving towards the prey.

I race my boat in toward the girl, grab her arm, and with one gigantic pull, send her tumbling into my boat. The shark is already heading back towards us.

"Hurry, Nate!" the girl yells. "The shark is on his way back."

"I've got this," I say, pushing the accelerator to high as we practically fly out of the water and towards the shore to safety.

The counselor runs towards us as we get out of the boat. "You did it, Nate! You did it! You saved our camper!"

"Thank you so much, Nate! Thank you," the girl sobs, looking up at me with tears in her eyes.

"Hey, Nathan, that's an awesome boat you just drew, but why are you just sitting here in this old rowboat doodling when we have a whole list of stuff to find?"

Charlie is standing over me. He seems a little annoyed. All of a sudden, he looks down and scoops a rock out of the water.

"Hey, here's a cool rock. Isn't that on your list?"

I pick up the rock and turn it around in my hands.

"Yeah," I say. "Thanks."

"That is one odd looking rock," Charlie remarks, taking it back to examine even further. "It sort of looks like a shark's tooth doesn't it? I wonder where that came from."

"Yeah...I wonder," I reply.

Chapter 10

At exactly 4:00, Tommy, Charlie, and I walk into the dining hall with our scavenger hunt finds. I think we did pretty well actually. By lunchtime we had located most of the items on the list, so we spent the rest of the afternoon working together, mostly just running up to counselors to see if any of them fit the descriptions on the list. We missed only three items: the four-leaf clover, the signature of the counselor whose middle name is Michael, and the hairband from a girls' counselor. I'm pretty sure no one found a four-leaf clover, so I'm not too worried about that one. As for the headband, none of the girl counselors were wearing headbands by the time we made it over to them, so I'm assuming they had already given them away to the other teams, and we asked everyone we could about their middle name—no Michaels. We did have that snakeskin though. I'm hoping it is enough to help us win.

Jerry says he will announce the winner of the scavenger hunt tonight. So far, Boys White is in third place. We won the kickball game and the soccer game, and we came in first on three out of ten relays. We came in second for everything else, except for the two events No-Neck did: basketball and tug-of-war. We lost both of those. We still had cheering, the talent show, t-shirts, and the results of the scavenger hunt after dinner. It was still anyone's game, but for now, we had a few hours to relax.

Of course, Matt wants us to spend the rest of the afternoon practicing our cheers and skits. I really don't see the point.

"Come on team! We need to get this together. I've been walking around to the other teams, and their stuff is pretty impressive. You don't want to get beat by a bunch of *girls* do you?"

"No," a few of the guys grumble.

"Good! Now let's line up and pretend that we're walking on stage."

Matt and the other counselors position the bench between the two trees that Tommy, Charlie, and I created. We also have a big make believe rock, and we painted a rusty old trashcan that Jerry said we could have. Tommy, Charlie, and I are toward the end of the line. No-Neck insisted on being last. He wants to be the one to say, "It's time."

One by one the boys on our team walk on to our pretend stage and sit on the bench. The person next to them asks, "Is it time?" They respond with a "No."

No-Neck, who is last, walks to the bench and sits down. Because I am the person before him in line, I ask him, "Is it time?"

He looks at me and says, "Yes, it's time."

We all move our hats to the other side. Hysterical ...not.

We do the skit perfectly on the first try, but Matt makes us repeat it three more times before we move on to cheers.

We should have stuck with the skit. In addition to our W-and-H-and-I-and-T-and-E cheer, Matt also made up one other cheer:

"We're Boys White and we came to fight. Blue and Red can go back to bed. We're fierce, we're proud, we'll never give in. Watch out other teams— we came to win. Our team is here, so don't come near, cause W-H-I-T-E spells victory!"

While we are saying the cheer, we are supposed to be forming a pyramid. The problem is, nobody can seem to do more than one thing at a time. If we don't say the words, we get the pyramid perfect. The moment we say the cheer, the pyramid is a mess. In the end, Matt decides that part of the group will do the pyramid, and the rest will say the cheer. I'm in the part that is cheering. Guess we can kiss those twenty points goodbye.

After dinner, we walk back over to the fields for the closing ceremonies. The stage now has a curtain attached to it. I suppose that is in preparation for the talent show. Jerry finds the opening in the curtain and walks out to the front of the stage. It is all very professional looking, well as professional looking as you can get when you are sitting in the middle of a field.

"Good evening, campers! Welcome to the final hours of the 45th annual Color War!" He waits as everyone screams and jumps around. Even I'm excited...excited for this all to be over with, that is.

"Mama T, can we bring out that leaderboard again?"

Once again, Mama T brings the board to the stage. I don't know why they just don't leave it there in the first place. It's not like anyone has been using the stage. Instead, poor Mama T has to carry it up and down the stage at the start and end of each event.

"Campers," Jerry says, "I honestly do not remember a better Color War competition than this one. The teams are so close together, anyone can win at this point. You kids are the most competitive and spirited group yet!"

"He says that every year," Charlie whispers in my ear.

"Right now all the teams are so close. Anyone can win. It all comes down to who wins tonight, so let's get started!" Jerry yells.

Everyone gets excited all over again. Mama T shushes everyone and starts talking. "Okay gang, I've been walking around the last few hours looking at all your team shirts. As you know, I get to pick the winner. This was not an easy decision, but the winning team for 20 points goes to...Girls Red!"

The Girls Red team rushes to the stage screaming and yelling. I immediately spot Abby at the front of the line showing off her shirt. What's the big deal? On the front, it says "Red Team Soars" and the back has extra fabric attached to it to look like wings. What is it with this camp and birds? That extra 20 points bumps Girls Red to second place from fourth place. There's no way Abby can finish ahead of me. I'll never hear the end of it.

"Congratulations girls!" Jerry says, as he nudges them back off the stage. "Now, it's time for my personal favorite part of Color War: the talent show! So without further ado, let's welcome to the stage Boys Blue!"

I watch as the boys blue team gets on stage and does some odd song and dance skit that I really don't understand at all. To be honest, Girls White and Girls Blue don't do much better. Neither does Boys Red. Maybe we actually have a shot at winning this competition.

Abby's team is up next. They have a few pieces of scenery that they put up to look like a backyard. In fact, it sort of looks like *my* backyard. The girls are standing around pretending to be having fun at a party. On the front of the stage, there is a girl playing horseshoes. She manages to get every horseshoe perfectly around the stake. Another girl walks on stage; only she is dressed to look like a boy, wearing a baseball cap and a plain t-shirt and shorts. She, I mean he, walks up to the girl.

(S)he says in a deep voice, "Hello, little girl, I'm a big strong boy, let me show you how to do that."

The girl replies, "Thanks, but I think I'm doing pretty well by myself."

"No," the girl/boy responds still with the deep voice, "I'm a boy, and I can show you how to do it better."

"I'm fine, *Nathan,*" the girl responds. She lifts her arm with the horseshoe and pretend hits the boy in the face.

The girl/boy then screams, "My eye, my eye, I have a black eye!" And runs off the stage crying. The audience is laughing hysterically.

Nathan?! Was that supposed to be me? Tommy elbows me, leans in, and says, "That was pretty funny, *Nathan*."

The girl on stage puts up both her arms as if to show off her muscles. All of the other girls surround her and yell, "Girl power—go red!" before they bow and walk off the stage.

I look around to see if anyone else has made the connection. No-Neck is staring directly at me and smirking. Just great. I turn back around.

"Thank you, girls. Last but not least, we have the boys white team."

I try to shake off the last skit, but all I can see when I walk on stage is Abby laughing and pointing at me. Matt and the other two counselors bring the benches to the stage, while Tommy, Charlie, and I set up the trees, the trashcan, and the rock. One final look around, and I leave the stage, lining up with the rest of my team.

As planned, one by one, we walk on stage. The person sitting next to us asks, "Is it time yet?" We each reply, "No." When No-Neck finally makes it on stage and sits next to me, I turn to him and ask, "Is it time yet?"

He is supposed to reply, "It's time." Instead, he just sits there, staring out at the crowd, saying absolutely nothing. Zilch.

So I ask him again, this time a little louder. "Is it time yet?"

Still nothing. I elbow him slightly. Again, he just sits there not doing or saying anything. I see Matt out of the corner of my eye. He is crawling behind the benches toward where No-Neck and I are sitting. When he reaches the spot directly behind No-Neck, he taps me to let me know I should try one more time.

By this time, everyone in the audience is giggling, not sure if this is part of the skit or not.

"Is it time yet?" I ask again, quite loudly this time.

"It's time!" says Matt's voice from behind the bench. We turn our hats to the other side. The audience has stopped giggling and now is just staring at us, clearly not getting the joke. Not that I ever thought it was funny to begin with. No-Neck still has not moved his body or his hat. I wonder if he is even alive. I decide to give him a little shove just to find out. As soon as I shove him, I realize I pushed a little too hard. He falls to the side, knocking the big tree over. It falls on Matt. As Matt tries to get up, the other tree comes tumbling down, falling directly onto Jerry who was caught off guard. Jerry then stumbles over the fake rock and falls face first into the curtain—bringing the whole cloth down on top of the audience. Finally everyone starts laughing, and I'm still not sure if they realize our skit went nothing like the way it was supposed to go.

Chapter 11

Jerry and Mama T manage to put the curtain back in place while No-Neck runs off the stage. Tommy and I carry away what is left of our trees, trying desperately not to look at the heckling crowd. What a disaster! That was even more embarrassing then Abby's skit.

"Well," Matt says when we gather together back in our spot on the field, "look at it this way—we still made everyone laugh didn't we?"

Leave it to Matt to find the bright spot, although he does looks pretty disappointed to me.

"This was all your fault," No-Neck says, looking straight at me.

"Me?" I yell, perhaps a bit too loudly. "You were the one who didn't say your line!"

"I was just waiting for the right moment. It's called *dramatic pause,* birdbrain. Actors win awards for that. Don't you know anything about theater?"

Theater? Since when is a camp skit equal to theater? Apparently, No-Neck forgot about the fact that someone else actually wound up saying his line and that he had completely froze on the stage. Dramatic? Yes. Theater? No. Besides, I was just making sure he wasn't dead. He should be thanking me.

Instead, he continues his barrage against me. "So what...you had to push me just to prove you're a tough guy now that the entire camp knows a *girl* actually gave you that black eye?"

"All right you two, that's enough. It was nobody's fault. Come on now, let's not forget we're a team here." Matt stands between No-Neck and me just to be sure we stop arguing. "Now listen up. We have a few minutes until they announce the winners of the talent show. After that, they'll go right into cheers. Let's move over to the side and practice one last time."

We follow Matt to find a clear patch of grass and wait for him to give us the signal to start. Charlie is part of the pyramid, and Tommy and I along with a few others are yelling the cheer. We all line up.

"And...go," Matt directs.

"We're Boys White and we came to win..."

"NO!" Matt yells. "Fight—we came to *fight*! You know, rhymes with *white*?" Matt sighs loudly. Sometimes I think Matt really regrets his decision to spend his summer as a counselor. "Let's try that again. Ready? Go!"

"We're Boys White and we came to fight. Red and Blue go back to bed."

"NO!" Matt yells, again. "Blue and *Red* go back to bed ...*Blue and Red*! It doesn't rhyme the other way!" Matt sits on the ground and puts his head between his hands. He sits for a good solid minute before he looks up. He pulls a few sheets of paper off his clipboard and hands them to Tommy with a pencil. "I give up," Matt says. "You guys will just have to write it down so you can read off the sheet when it's our turn."

Matt recites the cheer slowly so that Tommy can write it down. He then passes a blank piece of paper and pencil to the next kid so he can do the same. Eventually the paper and pencil makes its way down to me. I start writing, "We're Boys White and we came to fight. Blue and Red go back to bed."

"Okay campers, it's time to announce the winners of the talent show!" Jerry yells from the now completely put back together stage.

"Come on," Matt says and leads us back over to where we had been sitting before.

I look down at my unfinished cheer.

"I have to say, the skits this year were some of the best we've ever seen," Jerry says, as we settle back into our spot.

I lean over to Charlie and whisper, "Let me guess, he said that last year too?"

"Yup," Charlie replies.

I continue to copy the cheer off Tommy's paper while Jerry speaks, "Mama T, do we have the official results?" Jerry looks over to where Mama T had been standing just a few seconds earlier, but she is no longer there. "I guess she had to use the little girl's room," Jerry says shrugging his shoulders.

Everyone starts giggling and looking around for Mama T. Maybe it was finally time for Daisy to have her puppies.

"As I was saying, this year's skits were really amazing," Jerry continues, obviously trying to get control of the crowd once again, while stalling for time.

I turn around as someone taps me on the shoulder.

"Mama T? Aren't you supposed to be on stage or in the bathroom or something?"

"Nate, thank goodness I found you. I need you to come with me."

"Wow! Did we actually win the talent show? Hey Tommy, Charlie—come on—we have to go on stage. We won! Tommy? Charlie?" Where is everyone? Why is it so dark all of a sudden?

Standing up carefully, I bump into a plush folding theater seat. In fact, all around me are the same plush seats. Why am I in the middle of a dark theater? My neck suddenly feels itchy, and I notice I am no longer wearing my white team shirt, but rather a full black tie tuxedo. What in the world?

"Nate," Mama T says. I look over to her, but barely recognize her. She is wearing one of those fancy glittery dresses, and she even has on makeup. "You have to come quickly, we need your help!"

"What's going on?" I ask. On the stage at the front of the theater, there is a man giving a speech standing at a podium also wearing a tuxedo. It sounds like he is thanking everyone for winning some sort of award. Behind him a few steps back, is another man in a tuxedo. He looks strangely like Jerry, only with combed hair.

"Nate, we have to act quickly. After this speech, Jerry will announce the winner of 'Best Dramatic Pause.'"

Best Dramatic Pause? Not her too!

"The problem is, the envelope is actually a bomb. We received the threat just moments ago."

"Why don't you just make an announcement?" I ask. The solution seemed pretty simple if you ask me. "Or send word up to Jerry."

"Think about it, Nate. Jerry would not be able to stay calm. If word got out, it would cause a complete panic. People would be running and screaming toward one tiny exit. Nobody would get out safely. No, we have to stop him from opening that envelope without alerting anyone, or the entire building is going to be blown to bits! *You* have to stop him, Nate! We only have a few seconds. Please!"

As my eyes adjust to the darkness, I look around the theater. It is a packed house. Mama T is right. There is no way everyone would make it out safely. Soft music begins to play, signaling to the man on stage to wrap up his speech. The crowd applauds as he makes his way off the stage, carrying a trophy.

"I think I have an idea," I say as I sprint to the front of the stage.

"Hurry Nate, Hurry!" Mama T yells. I run as fast as I have ever ran in my entire life.

When I get to the side of the stage, I see the rope from the curtain hanging down. Just as I thought. I grab hold of it, and with all my strength, I shimmy up to the top where there is a small metal platform.

Holding the envelope, Jerry approaches the podium. It is difficult to hear what he is saying. He puts the envelope down and continues to talk. Everything starts to get a little fuzzy before my eyes as I process just how high up I truly am.

"Snap out of it," I whisper to myself. "Everyone is depending on you."

Jerry picks up the envelope once again.

Let's do this. I take a giant leap off the metal stand, holding tightly to the rope as it swings quickly through the air. I can hear people in the audience gasp. Still holding the unopened envelope, Jerry looks up at me as I swiftly approach.

"Nate?" he asks with a stunned look in his eyes.

I let go of the rope with one of my hands and pull the envelope away from Jerry. The envelope bounces off my hand and flies high into the air, turning in slow motion as it floats back towards the ground. The momentum of the rope causes me to swing back toward where Jerry is standing, but a person, wearing a black mask, runs on to the stage and attempts to grab the envelope, just as I swing by. I use my legs to push myself back toward Jerry once again.

"I'll take that," I say, as I swing back around. I grab the envelope just moments before it reaches the other person's hands. This time, I hold on to it tightly. The rope carries me to the far side of the stage. I jump off and quickly run through the exit door away from the building. Just as I run across the parking lot, a squad of cars with sirens and flashing lights comes to a halting stop. A man wearing a blue jumpsuit, with the words, "Bomb Squad" across the front of it, runs toward me from one of the cars.

"I believe this is what you're looking for," I say, as I hand him the envelope.

Mama T comes running out of the building towards us. She hugs me so tightly that I can barely breathe.

"Nate! Nate! You did it! That was amazing."

I see two police officers walking the mystery person, who is now in handcuffs, towards me. When they pull off his black mask, I immediately recognize him.

"No-Neck?" I ask, as he walks by smirking at me.

Shaking her head, Mama T looks at me. "Seems he was quite upset he wasn't nominated for the award for Best Dramatic Pause. He decided that if he couldn't win, nobody should win."

"Or live," the man from the bomb squad says. "Nate Rocks, you saved a lot of lives today. You are one rockin' hero."

"Nathan! Did you hear me? Abby's team won *again*," Tommy says, pulling the pencil out of my hand. "Stop drawing all over the paper that has our cheer on it. Matt wants us to line up; looks like we're going first. If we want a chance at winning this thing, we need to get this perfect. Man, I sure hope we don't bomb!"

"I think I know how to keep that from happening," I say smiling as I walk toward the stage.

Chapter 12

I've decided I like Color War after all. Our cheering went off without a hitch. We managed to get all the words right *and* make a perfect pyramid. Even No-Neck kept it together. I guess he's over his dramatic pause thing. Now that all the competitions are over, Matt finally seems a little more relaxed. He's even letting us do our own thing around the bonfire.

We start by singing some camp songs. Tommy, Charlie, and I are half singing and half goofing around. One of the counselors starts singing a song about a song that never ends. We basically just keep singing the same verse over and over again. Matt says it's supposed to be funny, but I'm bored after just the second round. Tommy and Charlie are singing at the top of their lungs. I look up to the stage and see Mama T carrying out her board and easel again. I elbow Tommy to get him to stop singing. He elbows me back, nearly knocking me into No-Neck who is sitting diagonal to me. Luckily, I miss him by a few inches.

Jerry is back on stage. I can see that his mouth is moving, but there is no way any of us can hear what he is saying as each verse of "The Song That

Never Ends" gets louder and louder. Finally, I see his fingers approach his lips, getting ready for that deadly whistle of his. I put my hands over my ears just in time. Within seconds, everyone stops singing.

"Okay now," Jerry says, wiping his forehead with his hat. That whistle must have taken a lot out of him. "The time has come we have all been waiting for...the crowning of this year's Color War champions!"

Everyone, including Charlie, Tommy, and me, once again goes nuts, jumping up and down and cheering. It is hard not to get excited this time, especially since I think we might have actually beat Abby in a competition. Their cheers were awful.

Jerry raises his hands to calm us down and begins speaking, "Well gang, it was not easy to decide who should win this year's cheering competition."

I lean over to Charlie. "Let me guess, we all had some of the best cheers he's ever heard."

"We had some of the best cheers this year that we have ever heard. Isn't that right, Mama T?" Jerry asks.

Mama T walks over to Jerry, nodding her head so enthusiastically, it looks as though her head might actually fall off her body and roll into the crowd.

"But only one team can be the winner. This year, the winner of the cheering competition is...Boys White!"

Matt and the rest of us jump up and down, screaming in joy. Even No-Neck seems excited.

"Mama T," Jerry continues, "can you update the

leaderboard for us? I think it's going to be a close race. In fact, I think this may be the closest race I've ever seen."

"At least since last year's Color War," Charlie says giggling.

"Okay everyone, it's down to just three teams: Girls Red, Boys Blue, and Boys White. Jerry, it looks like the winner of Color War will come down to the results of the scavenger hunt."

Talk about pressure! Jerry unfolds the piece of paper he had been holding. "Okay then, let's start with Boys Blue. Boys, can the members of your scavenger hunt team please stand up?" Jerry waits a few seconds while the three members of Boys Blue stand before continuing. "Out of the twenty items, you are missing 5 things: The counselor who doesn't like chocolate, the counselor who is afraid of spiders, the four leaf clover, the snake skin, and the bird feather. Not too bad, plus your score coming into this competition was pretty good as well. That leaves Boys Blue with a final score of 215 points."

The Boys Blue team cheers as Mama T updates the board.

"Next, we have Girls Red. Can the three scavenger hunt girls stand up?" Abby proudly stands up. I had no idea she also did scavenger hunt. "Your team really pulled it together at the end here, but unfortunately, you didn't do too well in the scavenger hunt. In fact, I'm not quite sure what you ladies were even doing yesterday. Working on your tan perhaps?"

We all start laughing, especially me.

"But, your team did have the highest score coming into the final competition. So even though you only retrieved three items..."

Jerry pauses as we all start cracking up again. He once again raises his hands so he can keep talking.

"...you still managed to squeeze ahead of Boys Blue with 220 points."

Now the Girls Red team jumps up and down screaming as Boys Blue take their seat.

"Quiet everyone, we still have one more team. Can the three boys from Boys White please stand?"

Tommy, Charlie, and I stand up grinning from ear to ear. We must have won. Jerry wouldn't have waited to announce us last if we hadn't won.

"Boys, I'm afraid out of the three teams, you came into the contest with the lowest score."

"Na—na," I hear Abby snicker from a few rows over. I look over to see her sticking her tongue out at me and making faces.

"It looks like the only way you can win this competition is if you found at least eighteen of the twenty items."

Suddenly, the smile on my face goes away. Eighteen? We only found seventeen items! That means Abby's team wins! How is this possible? They didn't even try to find any of the stuff. All they did was make some goofy looking shirts and put on a stupid skit.

"Mama T, do we have the official count for the number of items found by Boys White?"

"We sure do, Jerry. Boys White comes in with just..."

"Wait!" One of the counselors calls out from the crowd and pushes his way toward the stage. He runs over to Jerry and whispers in his ear, handing him a piece of paper. Mama T joins them.

"Kids," Jerry says, "I was about to announce that Boys White found only seventeen items..."

Girls Red starts jumping and screaming all over again.

"Girls!" Jerry yells, clearly running out of patience at this point. "Let me finish!" Jerry takes a deep breath before continuing, "It turns out that one of the items the Red Girls actually managed to hand in, was a four-leaf clover...*a drawing of a four-leaf clover*. While we never specified the item had to be an actual four-leaf clover, I'm afraid accepting drawings of items on the list takes the away from the purpose of the game: the hunt for the items— the *actual* items. We won't disqualify Girls Red due to the vagueness of the rule, but that means Girls Red only handed in two items, and Boys White wins Color War with their seventeen items!

"We won?!" Matt jumps up and starts racing toward the stage like a raging lunatic, knocking kids over as he creates his own path to the front, leaving our team behind. The rest of us are cheering and high-fiving. Even No-Neck is excited, although he has yet to high-five either Tommy, Charlie, or me. Jerry calls our team up to stage. Abby refuses to look at me as I walk right past her team. We all line up on the stage with Matt directly in front of us.

Mama T puts a championship medal around each of our necks as Jerry speaks, "Boys, let me be the first to congratulate you all on your exemplary performance today! Those of us who have been at Camp Spring Ridge awhile now, know that Boys White hasn't won a color war in many, many years. I didn't want to mention this fact before the competition started, but now that Boys White has broken the curse, what the heck."

Curse? Did he say curse? I look over at Charlie who just shrugs his shoulders. Apparently this secret goes back more than two years.

"It was the summer of 1976," Jerry begins. "The year of the Bicentennial. To celebrate, the camp decided to change the colors of Color War from our camp colors of orange, black, and yellow, to red, white, and blue, in honor of our nation's birthday. The teams were all set, the spirit was amazing, but one team outshone them all: Boys White. You see they had a camper on their team that everyone wanted. His name was Bob Ruttino—everyone called him the *Bobino*. The Bobino was amazing, winning almost every event and leading Boys White to a clear championship. The Bobino returned to camp and was put on Boys White the following year, leading to another sweep for the crown. By the fourth year, Boys White had won every Color War, and the other campers were getting tired of competing against the Bobino. The next year, the Bobino didn't return to camp. Boys White has not won a Color War since...until now! Congratulations once again to Boys White!"

We follow Matt's lead of raising our arms in victory as we march off the stage and back to our spot on the field around the bonfire. The whole 'Bobino' story still confused me.

"Hey Matt, did you know about the Bobino?" I ask, grabbing his arm as we sit down.

"Oh sure, Nathan. Jerry acts like it's some big secret, but everyone who's been here a while knows about the Bobino. It's just an old ghost story, no one really believes it."

"Gh—ghost story?" I ask. "What do you mean?"

"No, nothing," Matt says, "Don't you worry about it. Come on, let's celebrate our victory! The fireworks should be starting soon."

"Uh—sure," I mumble as I sit down.

"Hey, squirt, I hear you're wondering about that Bobino guy," No-Neck says to me. He sits down next to me with that smirk across his face. "From what I heard, the camp director at the time told him he couldn't come back to camp the next summer— said the other parents didn't want to send their kids there anymore if he was going to be there. I guess the other parents didn't want their kids thinking they were losers or something. So the camp director made a deal with another close by camp, and they agreed to take him there. Anyway, the Bobino got so mad, he ran away, but not before swearing to seek revenge on the camp. He was never heard from again, and it was rumored he died trying to sneak back into Camp Spring Ridge through the forest. I've heard some say they've seen his ghost roaming around in there...*and he doesn't look happy.*" No-Neck smacks his hands together, causing me to jump in my seat. He stands up and walks over to sit with some other kids.

I suddenly notice how dark it has gotten. The flames of the bonfire are our only light, casting shadows along the edge of the forest. At least, I hope they are shadows. I decide I need to continue reading the book Dad sent me as soon as we return to our cabin. I still needed to get through 367 more ways of how to ward off ghosts.

Chapter 13

Matt's been making us clean our bunks all morning. He wants everything to be perfect for visiting day this afternoon. I don't get the point. Our parents already know we are slobs. Plus, why bother even having a visiting day? We are all going home in two weeks anyway.

Mom's not coming today. She was going to drive up with Tommy's parents, but Grandma needed Mom to take her to visit some aunt I have never met before. In fact, I have never even heard of her. It seems like every time Mom writes to me she mentions a new relative I never knew existed. Where have all these people been the last ten years anyway, and why have I never heard of them? If you ask me, it all sounds a bit suspicious. I've got to remember to ask Grandma about these mysterious relatives when I get back home.

I finish putting away the last of my piled up clothing, as Matt calls us over.

"Looking good, Hawks! Just in time too. Your parents should be arriving any minute. See what we can accomplish when we put our minds to it and work as a team?"

We all grumble and nod our heads. The funny

part is, Matt did most of the work. Sure, I folded a few shirts, but for the most part we all stood around goofing off, while Matt walked around straightening things up. He even cleaned our bathroom, which was getting a little disgusting even for me. I wonder if Matt is going to come back to camp again next year. Color War champs or not, his enthusiasm seems to be dwindling each day.

"Knock Knock!"

I turn to the door to see Dad standing there. Tommy's parents are right behind him as are a bunch of other parents I've never met before.

"Dad!" I say, running up to him and giving him a hug. I don't even care who is watching, I'm just suddenly so happy to see a relative other than Abby.

The other kids all rush outside to find their parents.

Mr. and Mrs. Jensen come over and give me a hug as well. Tommy is already munching on cookies his mom brought. He is smiling ear to ear. I don't blame him. I've had his mom's cookies.

"Here, Nathan," Mrs. Jensen says, handing me one of the two boxes she is holding.

Awesome! She made me cookies also. This is a good day!

"Your mom wanted me to bring these for you. She knows they're your favorite! I have some for Abby too."

"Oh," I say, feeling that familiar forced grin I seem to have whenever someone starts talking about Mom's cooking. "Thanks."

I take the box from Mrs. Jensen. It feels like

it weighs about fifty pounds. I put it on the bed and carefully open it. Cookies *and* brownies. At least they look like cookies and brownies. I know from experience that they are actually bricks. The cookies, I think, are supposed to look like dinosaurs, or maybe they are fish with long tails? It's hard to tell.

"Yum!" I say, still with my goofy smile. "I'll have one later. I don't want to ruin my appetite for lunch."

"Did someone say lunch?" Charlie asks, walking back in the bunk with his Mom and Dad.

Charlie introduces us to his parents. They seem okay as far as parents go.

Matt walks over to shake all the parents' hands. "You guys can take your folks over to the dining hall anytime for lunch. I hear they are making a special meal in honor of our visitors today." Matt changes his perky voice to a whisper, "I'd stick with the sandwich station if I were you."

Dad laughs and smacks Matt on the back so hard that Matt goes flying and lands right on Joel's bed.

"Oops, sorry about that Matt. That reminds me. Nathan, did I ever tell you about the time Uncle Robert and I decided we wanted to become stuntmen?"

"You mean when Grandma caught you using her white couch cushions as your landing pads in the backyard?"

"Yeah," Dad says, staring out into nothingness, "Grandma told us if we wanted to live to see another year, we should pick another career choice. I still think I would have made a good stunt man though.

Anyway, I need to go get Abby before she thinks I forgot all about her."

Dad unclips a small compass from his belt hoop and hands it to me. "I have something for you, Nathan. I almost forgot to give it to you."

I take the compass and walk slowly in a circle watching as the needle changes direction. "Thanks, Dad," I say.

"I have to go find Abby, but when I get back, remind me to tell you about the time Uncle Robert and I got lost in the woods."

"Sure," I say, smiling. I put the compass into my pocket.

"Nathan, why don't you walk over to the dining hall with your friends, and I'll meet you there," Dad says, leaving me in the cabin with Tommy, Charlie, and their parents.

The dining hall is in complete chaos. Normally, bunks sit together, two tables for each bunk. Then, once everyone is seated, Luke, the head of the dining hall, calls each bunk up to get their food, one bunk at a time. Today is nothing like that. There are parents, grandparents, and siblings all pushing their way to get in and close to the food counters. You'd think these people hadn't eaten in weeks, maybe even months, by the way they are acting. Luke looks flustered, clearly unable to gain control. He finally walks over to the doorway and rings the bell. The bell can be heard loud and clear, all the way across camp, so you can imagine how loud it is when you are standing right next to it. No wonder Luke is so cranky all the time. He must have one giant headache from ringing that bell three times a day! The room instantly goes silent.

"Hi folks!" Luke says, trying to sound cheerful. "Welcome to Camp Spring Ridge! As you can see, we have a lot of people here today. Normally, we have our campers walk up to the counter to get their food, but since today is a special day, we are going to bring lunch to you. You'll notice that every table has a menu. Just check off the items you want. Our counselors will collect them and bring you your choices. So if everyone could just find a seat. Bon Appetite!"

Tommy, Charlie, and I along with Charlie's and Tommy's parents find an empty table.

"Shall we wait for your dad and Abby?" Tommy's mom asks.

"No, I think it's okay. We can start." I grab the menu from the center of the table and the pencil.

I list the options from the menu: cheeseburger, pizza, hot dog, and a turkey hoagie. Looks like the camp went all out today.

"Who wants to go first?" I ask.

"Cheeseburger," Charlie's dad blurts out. I put a check mark next to it on the menu.

"I'll have the pizza," Charlie's mom says, as we continue to go around the table.

Dad and Abby still haven't returned by the time Matt makes it over to collect our choices. I hand him the checked off menu anyway. Matt says they can order when they arrive.

"Hey, um, Nate, um, care to help me in the kitchen?"

"Sure, Matt." I get up from my seat. "I'm going to help with the food. I'll be right back," I tell everyone.

I walk through the swinging double doors of the kitchen, to find myself in what looks like a jungle. Where did the kitchen go? Where am I?

"Matt, where are we? Matt?"

I notice I am now dressed in khaki pants and a white t-shirt. I have on a khaki wide brim hat, and I am carrying an incredibly heavy backpack. A man I have never seen before is running towards me.

"Nate! Over here, quickly!"

I try to run towards the man, but the weight of my backpack slows me down. I throw it to the ground and meet the man as he runs towards me instead.

"Nate! The dinosaurs are heading toward camp. You've got to stop them!"

"Dinosaurs? Dinosaurs are extinct!" I reply. Clearly this man does not know what he is talking about.

"Nate, you've got to believe me! I'm with a group of scientists who live on the other side of the lake. We've been experimenting, trying to recreate dinosaurs for the last twenty years based on what we know about genetics, DNA, and cloning."

"I don't even know what any of that means," I say, still not sure I believe this guy. He has to be someone's parent playing with me.

"Trust me. There are dinosaurs on the other side of that lake! They escaped from their cages and are headed right for camp. And they look hungry!"

Suddenly, the ground rumbles as I hear a roar like no other roar I have ever heard in my life.

"Wha-what was that?" I ask, although I kind of already know the answer.

"That would be our T-Rex. Nate, I'm serious! We don't have much time!"

"But why me? You're the scientist!"

"Because you're Nate Rocks! Now please, we only have a few minutes. They're getting closer by the second!"

I can see the branches swaying on the row of trees just behind the lake. A large scaly head pops through and then opens its mouth to let out another colossal roar. There is a giant cage in the background with its door wide open. Whoa!

Think, Nate. Think! The backpack! I run back for it and drag it forward.

I open the backpack to see if there is anything in there that will help. Of course! I pull the cardboard box out of the bag and carefully remove the elastic bands that are holding the top secure.

The man leans over my shoulder to see what I am reaching for. "Cookies? Nate, this is no time for a snack!" the man yells.

Three more dinosaurs pop their heads above the trees. I ignore the man. I quickly find a stick on the ground in the shape of a "Y" and use one of the elastics that was wrapped around the box to make my own slingshot.

Carefully, I place a cookie into the slingshot. I gently, but firmly, pull back on the elastic. It is vital I get just the right amount of tension, or my entire plan will fail. I swiftly release the band and watch as the cookie flies through the air and into the T-Rex's mouth. He swallows in one gulp and proceeds to lick his lips.

He likes it! I move quickly now to send cookies flying even further behind the dinosaurs and closer to the cages. The first dinosaur turns around and retreats a few steps to search for the cookie. The other dinosaurs realize what is happening and move back slightly also.

I find another Y-shaped stick and make a second slingshot for the man standing next to me. "Here, you keep the dinosaurs distracted with cookies, and I'll start on the brownies."

I use the slingshot to pelt brownies across the lake. One by one, the dinosaurs start to fall to the ground after eating the treats.

"Are they ...dead?" the man asks.

"No," I reply. "They'll be okay. They just have bellyaches. You have about an hour before they'll be able to get back up."

A group of scientists run up to each dinosaur. They use ropes and pulleys to drag the beasts back into their giant cages. The men lock the dinosaurs securely inside.

"Nate!" the man says, as the other scientists come closer. "You did it! You kept the dinosaurs from invading your camp! That was genius!"

"Hey Nate, how did you know the cookies and brownies would stop them?" one of the scientists asks.

"I guess you've never had my mother's cooking," I reply with a grin.

"Roar!"

The sound startles me right out of my chair, as I see Abby cracking up!

"Aw, did the wittle dino scare Natie?" she asks, showing the entire table the picture of my dinosaur, as she sits down at the table. "Next time you decide to save the world with your drawings, can you not do it all over our lunch menu? How am I supposed to know what I want to eat now?"

"I've got some cookies and brownies back at my bunk you might like," I say with a smile.

Chapter 14

Dear Mom,

Sorry you couldn't make it to visiting day. To be honest, you really didn't miss much, although it was nice to see Dad. My friend Charlie's mom and dad came in first place in the three-legged relay race. Dad and Mr. Jensen were also in the race. They were partners, but fell over each other after one hop and never finished. Then Abby hit Mrs. Jensen in the face with an egg that she was supposed to be throwing to me in the egg toss competition. Abby says it's my fault. She says if I hadn't been standing so close to Mrs. Jensen, she wouldn't have hit her. If you ask me, Abby just has bad aim—or needs glasses—maybe both. Anyway, I hope you are having a nice time with Grandma and all of those relatives I previously knew nothing about. Perhaps we can have a family reunion when camp is over, so I can meet them. Miss you.

Love,

Nathan

P.S. Remember Mama T's dog Daisy? She finally had her puppies last week.

"Hey guys," Charlie calls over to Tommy and me, "come take a look at this!"

I stop packing my stuff for the bunk campout tonight to see what Charlie is looking at so intensely.

"I never noticed this before." He points to the wall behind where his pillow had been leaning. Carved into the wood are the words:

70's Rule ~ Go BW ~ I'll be back!—B.R.

"Do you think...?" Charlie starts.

"...70's? B.R.? Bob Ruttino! I'll bet this was the Bobino's bunk!" Tommy says excitedly.

"I think so too! BW—Boys White! Yes! It has to be!" Charlie agrees.

I step in a little closer. "Are you sure?" I ask, not quite certain of how I feel about sharing the same cabin as the late great Bobino.

"Definitely!" Tommy states, "Who else would have written something like that?"

"Or signed it B.R.?" Charlie adds.

What if No-Neck was right? What if the Bobino didn't want to leave camp, but was forced to? Did his ghost really come back to live in the woods to seek revenge against us?

"Come on boys," Matt says, looking in our direction, "let's finish getting our stuff together. We still have to pitch our tents for our big campout. I want to make sure we have everything set up before it gets too dark. We are going to have so much fun tonight. Now make sure you have warm enough clothes with you. It can get pretty chilly out there."

No-Neck looks up from his duffle bag and rolls his

eyes. I have to admit, I'm kind of with him on this one. I mean, haven't we *been* camping for the past five weeks already? One room cabin with no heat or air-conditioning, sleeping bag on a flimsy metal bunk, water spigot outside the front door...yup feels like camping to me! Being out in a tent in the field is really no different. What's the big deal? If we forget something or have to go to the bathroom, all we have to do is just go back to the cabin. Charlie even told me that some of the kids even sneak back to the bunk to sleep.

Matt says this is all part of the overnight camp experience. Every few nights, a different bunk gets to pitch tents and sleep out in the fields. Tonight it's our turn. I head back over to my bed and grab my pillow, knocking Dad's book to the floor.

Without giving it much thought, I pick it up and throw it into my duffle bag. I can always read with my flashlight if I can't sleep.

Our campsite looks like something out of a bad war movie. Not that I've seen that many, but Dad watches them, and he lets me stay to watch as long as Mom's not home to make a fuss about me watching something violent. In one movie I saw, the campsite had been attacked. All the tents were lopsided and falling down. Matt thinks we did a great job, but if you ask me, our site looks exactly like the site in the movie...only with just two tents. Hopefully neither of the two tents we have set up will fall down in the middle of the night.

Tommy, Charlie, and I unroll our sleeping bags next to one another in one of the tents and go join the others who are already sitting by the campfire. Matt plays his guitar as we sing songs and cook food on sticks over the fire. Darkness slowly creeps in, until the campfire becomes our only source of light.

Matt suddenly stops playing and looks around at our group as we toast the last of our marshmallows.

"Dark out here, isn't it?" Matt says in this weird voice that I think is supposed to sound scary. Instead it sounds like someone trying to do a bad impersonation of a vampire or something. "I sure hope Chief Spring Ridge doesn't show up."

Charlie leans over to Tommy and me. "Oh boy, here we go." Charlie had told both of us before we left the cabin that every year at the campout the counselors always tell the same story, trying to scare the campers. He said it might actually work, if the story was even remotely scary, but he says it's more ridiculous than scary. I sure hope Charlie is right.

"Who's Chief Spring Ridge?" Walt asks, sneering. Guess he's heard this story before too and feels the same way as Charlie. I settle back, feeling pretty confident there is nothing to worry about.

"Well," Matt continues in that weird voice again, "It all started hundreds and hundreds of years ago—back before Columbus came to America—back when the Indians lived on this land. The piece of land we now call Camp Spring Ridge was actually an Indian Reserve, the home to a small yet very powerful tribe. The tribe's chief, Chief Spring Ridge, was one of the most respected chiefs in all the land. To protect the land, the tribesman put up two totem poles, which still sit at the entrance to our camp. Chief Spring Ridge eventually moved his tribe, but before they left, he proclaimed a section of this land as a sacred burial ground, a place for his tribe members to be buried as their spirits pass to their much desired after life, their true home. It has been said that some of the spirits were unable to find their way home and instead wander aimlessly around the burial ground."

Charlie whispers in my ear, "In fact, the very spot we are sitting is where they are buried."

"In fact," Matt says, lowering his voice to an even weirder voice, "the very spot we are sitting is where they are buried."

Mark and Walt make sounds pretending they are farting while the rest of us roll on the ground laughing.

"All right," Matt says, returning to his normal voice. "That's enough. It's getting late. I'm going to see if I can't get these tents a little more secure."

Mark sits up straight and begins talking. "Forget the Indians, the one you really want to watch out for is Old Man Withers."

I look over to Charlie and mouth the words, "Old Man Withers?"

He shakes his head no and shrugs his shoulders.

All the rest of the kids stop goofing around and lean in around the fire to listen to Mark.

"About a hundred years ago, back when the camp first opened, this entire area was all woods. In order to clear out enough space to make a camp, all the trees needed to be cut down. The owner of the camp hired this guy named Wayne Darby to take down all the trees."

"Darby?" Lee asks, "That's your last name."

"That's right," Mark says. "Wayne Darby was my great-great grandfather. That's how I know this is a true story." The flames suddenly begin to cast strange shadows over Mark's face as he leans into the fire and continues speaking.

"For a month before the camp opened," Mark says, "Wayne came with his axe and cut the trees one by one. Only there was a problem...the camp didn't actually own the land. Seems a farmer named Max Withers was the owner. It turned out that Max had a history of breaking the law, and the police had finally caught up with him. They threw him in jail, where he grew old and eventually went crazy. His family sold the land to the camp without the old man's consent. When Old Man Withers found out about the sale, he began to dig and dig and dig. Dug himself a hole right through the prison floor and escaped the jail. The prison guards said they never saw anything like it before. Old Man Withers was determined to reclaim his land, and nothing was going to stand in his way."

"What happened?" Tommy asks.

"Well, according to my great-great grandfather, Old Man Withers did make it back to camp. Wayne had already cleared out the fields and the area around the lake. He was just about to chop the trees that now make up the forest." Mark points over to the dark wall of trees. "Old Man Withers was so angry when he saw how many trees were gone, he grabbed the axe right out of Wayne's hands and tried to attack Wayne with it. Luckily, Wayne got away, but not before Old Man Withers vowed to destroy anyone who came near his forest again."

"What happened to Old Man Withers?" Lee asks.

"Don't know," Mark says, standing up to brush the grass off his legs. "That's one part of the story my great-great grandfather never told anyone. He died way before I was even born. Guess we'll never know."

"Okay guys, we are all set," Matt says, as he pops his head out from around a still lopsided tent. "It's almost 11:00 already. Time to hit the sack."

Because our tent is the bigger of the two, we have seven kids: me, Tommy, Charlie, Lee, Walt, Danny, and Joel. Jason, Mark, Matt, and No-Neck are in the other tent.

It is still dark in the tent when my eyes suddenly pop open. I look over at the other kids. They're all sound asleep. I wonder what time it is. Whatever time it is, it is definitely not morning. I close my eyes and try to fall back to sleep.

Chop. Chop. Chop. The sound is in the distance, yet annoying enough to keep me awake. I look over and see Danny starting to stir. He opens his eyes, sits up, and looks right at me.

"Did you hear that?" he asks.

I nod.

Chop. Chop. Chop. The sound seems to be getting louder, waking just about everyone in the tent. We all sit up and turn our flashlights on.

"What do you think it is?" Tommy asks.

"I—I don't know," I reply.

"It almost sounds like...," Charlie stops mid-sentence.

"Sounds like what?" I ask.

"Sounds like an axe," Danny replies quietly.

"What if it's the ghost of Mark's great-great grandfather?" Lee asks.

"Or Old Man Withers!" whispers Walt, in an excited tone. "You heard what Mark said. He was really angry! And now he's got an axe!"

"I don't want to die!" Joel whimpers.

"Me either!" Charlie cries.

Chop. Chop. Chop. The sound is the loudest it has been yet.

"I'm scared," Danny yells.

"Where's that mess kit Mama T dropped off earlier tonight?" I ask, feeling surprisingly calm.

"What's a mess kit?" Tommy asks.

"You know, all those pots and pans?" At the time, I didn't know what Mama T was thinking, giving us a box of old pots and pans. It's not like we were about to cook up a gourmet meal over the fire. We barely managed to cook our hotdogs on sticks. Half of them wound up falling into the fire.

Charlie opened the tent flap just enough to reach the box and pull it inside. "Quick," I instruct, "everyone grab two pans and bang them together as loud as you can!"

The noise is deafening, but we keep at it—clanging and banging.

"Stop! Stop! ENOUGH!!"

Matt is standing in the doorway of our tent, not

looking happy at all.

"What in the world is going on in here?" he yells.

"We're scaring off the ghosts," I say. I grab the book Dad sent me and open to page 35. "See?" I hand Matt the book.

"Number 54: Ghosts do not like noise. Find any nearby objects and bang them together as loudly as you can. Your ghosts will surely disappear into the night."

All of a sudden, we hear Mark and No-Neck cackling next to our tent.

"I think I found your ghosts," Matt says, pulling them inside. Mark and No-Neck are still hysterical. "Do you boys have anything to say?"

"*I don't want to die,*" No-Neck mimics in between laughs.

"*I'm scared,*" Mark whines through giggles.

"Fine. You boys just bought yourselves an extra week doing dining hall duty. Last week of camp too. Please, can we all just get some sleep now?" Matt leaves our tent with No-Neck and Mark sulking behind him.

"Thanks, Nathan," Danny says. "That book is pretty cool."

"Yeah," I say. I grab a pen from my bag and put a big circle around number 54.

Chapter 15

"Nate, wake up, Nate! Nate!"

"Huh?" I open my eyes, forgetting where I am for a moment. "Matt?"

"Nate! You've got to wake up!"

"What's going on?"

"I need your help! The boys from my tent are missing. I overheard them talking earlier about heading to the forest tonight, but I didn't think they were serious!"

I shake my head to try to wake myself up. "Jason, Mark, and No-Neck went to the forest? Why would they do that?"

"Nate! You've got to find them. It's dangerous in there. Remember you asked me about the Bobino at the end of Color War? Well, I maybe didn't tell you the whole story."

"What do you mean?"

"Um, I've heard things...things about his ghost. I can't say for sure, but it's not pretty. You have to find those boys. The forest is not safe for them!"

"M-m-me? Why me?"

"Why because you're Nate Rocks—of course! There is no better ghost hunter around. Now please, there is no time to waste!"

I step out of the tent. "You're coming with me, right Matt? Matt?"

I look around but there is no sign of Matt. In fact, the tents, the field—everything—gone. Instead, I am standing in pitch darkness. I turn on my flashlight to see only a thick dark forest on all sides.

"Hello?" I ask, not quite softly, but not quite loudly either.

"Hello?" I ask again, louder this time.

"We're here!" The faint voices rustle through the trees. The voices are too far away to determine if they sound familiar. What if it's actually the Bobino yelling for me, trying to lure me into a trap? I've got to find out.

"You come to me," I yell. I then run quickly to hide behind a large boulder. I find a good size stone and throw it away from myself, hopefully to make whoever it is think I am really located in the opposite direction. Suddenly, I see Mark, Jason, and No-Neck run in the direction of the stone.

"Psst," I whisper loudly. "It's me Nate." The three boys run toward me and hide behind the rock.

"Nate! Thank goodness you came to save us," Jason says. "We're lost. You've got to help get us out of here!"

"You can get us out of here, right Nate?" Mark asks with pleading eyes.

"Forget him," No-Neck says, "I can get us out of here." He glares at me. "Now we're just stuck with another person. I'll bet he's scared too. He's just going to slow us down."

Mark puts his arm around my shoulder. "Leave

him alone. We need him. *You've* only been walking us in circles for the past hour. *He* can get us out of here. Right Nate?"

"Uh—sure," I answer, not exactly with the most convincing voice.

"All right, hot shot," No-Neck says, "so what's your plan?"

To be honest, I didn't have a plan. Up until just a few minutes ago, I was toasty snug in my sleeping bag, fast asleep. The breeze runs a chill down my spine, and I put my hands in my pockets to keep warm. My fingers hit a piece of cold metal— the compass! I quickly pull it out and shine my flashlight on it.

"A compass! You're a genius, Nate! A genius!" Jason says.

"Come on, we need to go east." I shine my flashlight and start walking, leading the way.

"THERE IS NO ESCAPE..."

I freeze. Mark, Jason, and No-Neck all bump into me, and we fall to the ground.

"Did you hear that?" No-Neck asks. We all nod, unable to speak. "I'll bet that's Old Man Withers!"

"Nah," Mark says. "I made that whole story up."

"ONCE YOU ENTER THE FORBIDDEN FOREST, YOU ARE HERE FOREVER..."

"The Bobino!" I whisper.

"You mean?" Mark asks.

"Yes," I reply. "It has to be him."

"What are we going to do, Nate?" Jason asks, his voice shaking as he speaks.

I pull the worn book out of my back pocket for

the second time tonight and flip through the pages. This situation is going to take more than a few pots and pans.

"Here it is." I hold my flashlight over the page: *Number 347: Have a conversation with the ghost. Explain who you are and why you are there. If that doesn't work, see Number 1,001.* I flip to number 1,001: *Run!* "This has to work," I say quietly, as I look over at Mark, Jason, and No-Neck.

"So let's hear it, hot shot. What do we do now?" No-Neck asks.

"We're going to have a séance," I say.

"A what?" asks Jason.

"It means he wants us to sit around and hold hands. No thanks, I'll be over here," No-Neck says, as he hops on top of the large boulder.

I look to Jason and Mark. "A séance is where we talk to the ghost, let him know we're not here to hurt him. We tell him we understand, and we're on his side," I explain. "The first thing we need to do is build a fire."

"But we don't have any matches," Jason says as he quickly collects logs and sticks and throws them in a pile on the ground."

"We don't need matches," I say. I take two sticks and rub them together continually until a flame appears. I throw the flame onto the sticks. A roaring fire appears.

"Wow," Jason says. "How'd you do that?"

"He's Nate Rocks," Mark answers. "He can do anything. What next, Nate?"

"Okay," I instruct, "we need to sit around the fire

and then start a conversation with him."

"Do we need to hold hands?" Jason asks.

I look over at No-Neck just sitting on the boulder, pretending not to watch us. "No. We don't."

"How about garlic? Shouldn't we be wearing garlic or something?"

"That's to keep vampires away, not ghosts," No-Neck says. He jumps off the rock and sits with us by the fire.

"Okay then, let's get started." I close my eyes and begin speaking:

"Hello Great Bobino. We are sorry to have invaded your woods."

"WHAT DO YOU WANT?" the rumbling voice responds.

Jason and Mark look terrified. Even No-Neck looks a bit scared. I close my eyes and continue talking in a calm, even-toned voice. "Sir, we are campers at Camp Spring Ridge. In fact we are Hawks, the very same bunk you were once in. We found your initials carved into our cabin. Everyone there really looks up to you. You were a hero...a legend even."

"REALLY?" the voice asks, softening up a bit.

"Oh absolutely," I continue. "Actually, you'll be happy to hear that Boys White won Color War this year, in YOUR honor." I wink at the others.

"Nice touch," Mark whispers, leaning over to me.

"YOU DON'T SAY...YOU MEAN THEY DON'T ALL HATE ME?"

"Hate you? Why would they hate the Great Bobino? Everyone loves you. In fact, I've heard talk about them changing the name of the camp to Camp Bobino."

Shoot, that claim may have been a bit too much, but the Bobino doesn't seem to notice.

"WHY THAT'S VERY NICE." Bobino pauses and then adds, "BUT WHAT ARE YOU BOYS DOING IN *MY* WOODS?" His voice is getting loud again.

"Sir, I'm afraid that's just a terrible mistake. We didn't mean to disturb you, honest. We got lost. We'd really like to return to our bunk."

"WELL..."

"Just think of what a hero you would be if we told everyone how you helped us get out."

"YOU WOULD DO THAT? EVEN AFTER I TRIED TO SCARE YOU BOYS?"

"Of course! You're the Great Bobino!"

"The Great Boobino is more like it," No-Neck mumbles, unfortunately loud enough for the Bobino to hear.

"NOT SO FAST!" Bobino hollers, causing the entire ground to shake. "YOU! THE ONE WITH NO NECK!"

"Y-y-y-yes sir?"

"I DON'T THINK I LIKE YOUR ATTITUDE, BOSSING PEOPLE AROUND AND MAKING FUN OF THEM ALL THE TIME."

"Y-yes sir."

"NOW I THINK YOU OWE ME AN APOLOGY, AND WHILE YOU ARE AT IT, YOU CAN APOLOGIZE TO YOUR FRIENDS HERE ALSO."

"I'm very sorry," No-Neck says looking down at the ground. "To all of you."

"THAT'S BETTER."

Suddenly, and without warning, a path appears. A warm glow radiates down the path directing us to the edge of the woods and back into the fields.

"Thank you, Mr. Bobino," I say, letting the breath out that I didn't realize I had been holding, "you rock."

"NO, NATE. *YOU* ROCK!"

I stand up and smile. Jason and Mark throw stones on the fire to put out the flames. No-Neck is already half way down the path, running toward the light.

"Nathan—are you listening? I can't fall asleep with that flashlight in my eyes," Tommy says. "Why are you drawing pictures in that book your Dad sent you? What if we need to ward off ghosts again? We won't be able to read it!"

"Oh don't worry," I respond, "I'm pretty sure we won't have anymore ghost sightings tonight."

Chapter 16

Our cabin has an odd stillness to it today. Or maybe it's just the stench of dirty socks that have been wedged between the shelves for the past six weeks. Something definitely seems different today. I suppose it has something to do with the fact that today is our last day here at Camp Spring Ridge. I hate to admit it, but I think I may actually miss being here. I might even ask if I can come back next summer.

I mean, put aside the regular kickball games, the occasional unexpected dunk in the pool, the bug bites, and the stinky bathrooms; this place is okay. Even No-Neck has been nicer to me, although I suspect it has something to do with the campout last week. Plus, I got to spend every day with Tommy, met Charlie and Lee, didn't have to eat Mom's cooking, and barely saw Abby the entire summer. Overall, I would say the pluses definitely outweighed the minuses.

Packing up all my stuff is no easy task. Matt wants us to have all of our things ready to go when our parents arrive. He says it's camp policy, but personally I think it's because he's ready for us to all go home. I look at the mounds of clothing, towels, sheets, and other assorted items piled on my bed. How the heck did Mom fit everything into these two duffle bags? Surely, I'm missing something here. Maybe I actually had three bags?

"Hey Tommy," I ask. "Do you have one of my bags up there?"

Tommy leans over the top bunk and says, "I don't think so. I just have my two."

"Well, do you have any extra room? I don't think all my stuff is going to fit."

Tommy jumps off his bunk and examines my pile.

"You're fine," Charlie says, walking over to my bed. He picks up one of my already neatly folded t-shirts and shakes it back out. "All you have to do is just ball each item up as tightly as possible." He crumples the shirt into a tight ball. "Then you just shove it into the bag like this." He pulls the bag open and pushes the balled up shirt tight into a corner. "Trust me, it works every time."

"Cool, thanks," I say and proceed to unfold all of my shirts. Sure enough, balling and mushing everything together works perfectly. My two bags are packed and ready to go.

"Gather round, Hawks," Matt calls. We all stop what we are doing and walk over to Matt. He is standing at his bunk with a sad look on his face. His bags are also packed. I wonder if his parents are coming to get him as well. "Well," he begins, flipping the pages of his clipboard. I never did get a chance to peek at that thing. I'm still not sure exactly what is so important about all of those papers or why Matt always had to flip through them every time he spoke. "I just wanted to say it has been a great summer. I've really enjoyed getting to know all of you. I hope you all had a terrific summer too. I know I will be back next summer, and I hope all of you will be back as well."

Matt extends his arm out and into the middle of our little group circle. Nobody else seems to know what to do, so we just stand there in silence. Charlie puts his arm out as well, his hand covering Matt's and nudges me, so I reach my arm out and put my hand over Charlie's. Everyone else follows, and Matt yells, "Go Hawks!" We all raise our arm out of the circle. Matt looks around at us. He looks as if he may start to cry. Finally, after what seems like forever, he unzips his bag and puts the clipboard away.

We go outside to wait as the line of cars belonging to parents starts to make its way down the road leading to the bunks. I can see Mom's van toward the middle of the line. It's pretty hard to miss it. Waving fast and furious, Mom is practically hanging out of the car. Luckily, the other kids don't seem to notice as their own parents' cars pull up.

"Nathan!" Mom yells, barely waiting for Dad to park before she jumps out of the van. She nearly knocks me over as she hugs me. "How is my sweet little boy?"

"Um fine," I answer, trying to escape her grasp and make sure no one else is listening all at the same time.

"Tommy," Mom says releasing me to give him a hug as well. "How are you?"

"Fine, Mrs. Rockledge."

Dad comes over and pats me on the back. "Good to see you again, son."

"Thanks Dad, you too. Everything is all packed."

"Bill," Mom says to Dad, as she finally lets me free, "I should go find Abby while you pack up the car with Nathan's and Tommy's things."

"Okay," Dad says. "We'll see you in a bit."

Mom gives me one more big hug and kiss, "I sure did miss you, Nathan. You look thin to me. Did you eat okay?"

"Sure, Mom."

"Abby wrote to me about the awful camp food here," she whispers. "Well, don't you worry, you'll be eating my home cooked meals again in no time!"

"Great," I say, trying hard to look happy. "Can't wait."

"Okay, well I better get going. I don't want to keep Abby waiting. See you boys soon."

We watch as Mom crosses the field towards the girls' camp. Mama T drives up and stops her van in front of our bunk.

"Ahoy there, Hawks," she says, wearing the same straw hat she had on the first day of camp. She opens the van's sliding door and pulls several booklets out of a box that is resting on the seat. Jerry, who is with her, gets out of the passenger seat and shakes hands with all the parents.

"Here you go!" Mama T hands us each a book. On the cover there is a picture of the totem poles and sign that are at the entrance of the camp. Inside the booklet, are photos taken from the summer, including the one of Boys White standing on the stage while receiving our winning medals.

"Your official camp yearbook," Mama T says. "Well, not really a yearbook since you weren't here all year. More like a 'season book.' No that doesn't sound right either. Maybe a 'summer book?' Hmm, maybe we should call it a yearbook after all. Or..."

"Let's just call it a memory book," Jerry interjects. "There are lots of great memories from the summer in this here book to help keep Camp Spring Ridge with you all year round. Plus some blank pages in the back where you can write each other's names and phone numbers. I hope you've all had a great summer and will keep in touch!"

Charlie immediately hands his book to me. "Nathan, will you write in your phone number?"

Dad hands me a pencil. "Here you go, Nathan. I'm going to go into the cabin to grab your stuff."

"Okay, thanks," I say, taking the book and pencil. I hand Charlie my book for him to do the same.

"I'll be right back. I think I have an extra pen in my duffel bag," he says, as he follows Dad into the cabin.

I'm just about to write my phone number down when I hear Mama T let out a shriek.

"Help! Daisy's puppy! Help!"

I turn towards Mama T. Her van is starting to roll down the road all by itself. I look around, but it seems that everyone else has already gone back into the cabin. She runs over to me and grabs my shirt, "Nate! One of the puppies is in the back seat in a box! My van is headed right for the lake! You've got to help me stop it."

Sure enough, Mama T's van had veered off the road and was headed straight for the lake.

"Please, Nate! Please!"

I take off running toward the lake. The van gains momentum as it rolls down the hill, yet it is still going slow enough for me to reach it. If I can just get inside the van, I can grab the box with the puppy and jump out. Yes, Mama T's van will still go in the water, but at least the puppy will be safe. I easily reach the door handle, but no matter how hard I tug, the door will not open. Are you kidding?

"Hurry, Nate!" I hear Mama T yell from behind me. "Hurry!"

Realizing that I need a different plan, I let go of the door. *Think Nate!* I have to stop this van before it goes into the lake. I have to save Daisy's puppy!

"I have an idea," I whisper to myself, panting as I continue to jog along next to the van. I break away from the path and sprint to the sports shed on the edge of the field. Quickly, I pull the door open and rummage through a pile of balls, nets, and cones until I find what I am looking for: the tug of war rope from Color War!

I run back to catch up to the van and secure the rope around the van's old and rusted trailer hitch.

I pull on the rope as hard as I can, trying to get the van to stop, but it is still moving, pulling me along with it. The edge of the lake is only a few feet away. The back of my heels are digging in the dirt creating a path behind me. If I can't stop this van, it will be in the water in just a few seconds.

Then what will I do? *Pull it together Nate—you can do this—you've managed to escape snakes and dinosaurs and sharks. Surely, you can stop a van!*

I try to catch my breath and count down, concentrating as hard as I can: "three, two, one— PULL!"

Suddenly, I feel more tension on the rope. The van is slowing down! I turn around to see a man I have never seen before holding the back of the rope and helping me pull. The van finally comes to a complete stop just as the front tires enter the water's edge.

I still cannot get the doors open. I find a rock and smash through the front window of the van. Climbing inside, I grab the terrified puppy. He is barely bigger than my hands.

The man helps to pull me out of the van. Mama T comes running up to me and hugs me, nearly crushing her dog.

"Thank you, Nathan! Thank you!" She cries. "You saved Daisy's puppy!"

"Don't thank me," I say, looking at the man. "I couldn't have done this by myself. Thank you sir," I say to the man. "If it weren't for you, the van would surely have gone into the water."

"No, you were the true hero," he says. "I just gave it a little extra muscle. You were the one who set it all in motion. You should be very proud of yourself."

"Sorry about your window, Mama T," I say, still holding the puppy.

Putting her arm around my shoulder, Mama T says, "Oh don't be silly. I'm sure Jerry can figure something out with a little duct tape."

"Nathan! Are you okay?" Mom and Abby run across the field toward me. Dad, along with the rest of my bunk, is running from the direction of the cabin.

"I'm fine, just helping Mama T out with something," I say smiling, stroking the dog's soft fur.

"Oh now, your boy's being awfully modest here," the man still standing next to me says. "He just kept this van from going into the lake and single-handedly saved this puppy's life!"

"Well, not single-handedly," I say, looking at the man.

"Oh, all I did was give it a little tug. Your son did all the hard work." The man puts his hand out for Dad to shake. "I'm Bob."

"Bill," Dad says, shaking his hand.

"Nathan," Mama T says, "I just had the best idea! Why don't you keep this puppy? To thank you, that is, if it's okay with your parents."

"Can I, Mom? Dad? Please??"

"Well..." Mom says. "Why don't you let Dad and I talk about it while you say goodbye to your friends."

"Okay," I say, as we walk back up the hill toward my bunk.

I find my season/memory/summer yearbook and continue to pass it around to collect phone numbers as the adults mingle with each other.

"You forgot me," No-Neck says, grabbing the book out of my hand. He writes quickly and hands it back to me.

I look down at his handwriting: *Bobby Ruttino, Jr. 555-0124.*

"Bobby Ruttino?" I glance up. The man who had helped save the puppy is now standing next to No-Neck—I mean Bobby—with his hand on his shoulder.

"Yup," Bobby, Jr. says with a big smile on his face.

"You mean this is...He's...?" Unable to speak, I stare at Bobby's dad.

"Nathan," Mr. Ruttino says, "so nice to meet one of Bobby's friends. I hear you were on the boys white team together. That's my old team you know. Congratulations on your win, and again, what you did just now was amazing. I hope we'll see you next summer." He pats my back and turns to Bobby. "You finish up your goodbyes. I'll be waiting in the car."

I close my eyes for a split second as the Bobino walks over to his car. Then I look back down at the paper to make sure I'm not seeing things. "You made that whole story up?" I ask Bobby, Jr.

Mom and Dad walk over to me carrying the puppy. "Nathan," Mom says, "we've decided you can keep the puppy."

"See you next summer, squirt," Bobby, Jr. says. "You're okay." He winks at me and walks towards his dad's car.

"Oh sure, I ask for a puppy for years and the answer is always *noooo*, but all Nathan has to do is run after some old rickety van and poof, he gets a puppy." Abby gets into Mom's van and slams the door.

"Thanks, Mom! Thanks, Dad!" I give each of them a hug and take the puppy into my arms. He gives me a little puppy lick on my nose. "I think Bobino is going to love his new home."

"Bobino?" Dad asks, "Where did you come up with that name?"

"Dad," I say, reaching my free arm up around his shoulder as we walk toward the car, "Did I ever tell you about the time I went away to summer camp?"

Nate Rocks:
Part Super-Hero, Part All-Star Athlete,
Part Rock-Star...Part Fourth-Grader?

Read the Book That Started It All!

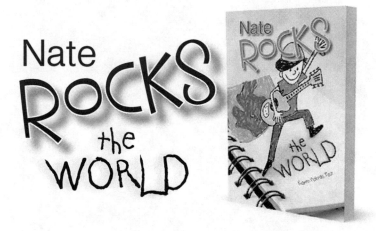

Life as a fourth-grader can be hazardous—after all, there are science projects to deal with, Halloween costumes to create, and family vacations (with a big sister along—ugh!) Armed only with his imagination and his wits, Nathan Rockledge navigates the perils of the fourth-grade in style, to emerge, heroic, as **Nate Rocks!**

Join Nathan, Tommy, Abby, and Lisa for more fun and hilarious adventures!

CPSIA information can be obtained at www.ICGtesting.com
Printed in the USA
LVOW041710250512

283341LV00003B/90/P

9 780984 860814